Rafiq. A r

He was very good-looking. His face was a composition of high cheekbones, straight nose and square jaw that came dangerously close to male perfection. Broad shoulders and a wide chest fit his tall body. His sinfully expensive suit highlighted lean, masculine strength.

She's always thought Texas cowboys were the standard of male appeal. Prince Rafiq Hassan just upped the benchmark. She had the heart palpitations, weak knees and sweaty palms to prove it.

"May I come in?" he asked.

"Of course." She pulled the door wide and stood back, allowing him entrance.

He looked at her. "You've changed your clothes."

She followed his glance to her bare feet, jeans and Don't Mess With Texas T-shirt. When she met his gaze again, it contained a spark of…something she didn't understand. And she could only think of one word to describe his black eyes.

Smoldering.

Dear Reader,

My, how time flies! I still remember the excitement of becoming Senior Editor for Silhouette Romance and the thrill of working with these wonderful authors and stories on a regular basis. My duties have recently changed, and I'm going to miss being privileged to read these stories before anyone else. But don't worry, I'll still be reading the published books! I don't think there's anything as reassuring, affirming and altogether delightful as curling up with a bunch of Silhouette Romance novels and dreaming the day away. So know that I'm joining you, even though Mavis Allen will have the pleasure of guiding the line now.

And for this last batch that I'm bringing to you, we've got some terrific stories! Raye Morgan is finishing up her CATCHING THE CROWN series with *Counterfeit Princess* (SR #1672), a fun tale that proves love can conquer all. And Teresa Southwick is just beginning her DESERT BRIDES trilogy about three sheiks who are challenged— and caught!—by American women. Don't miss the first story, *To Catch a Sheik* (SR #1674).

Longtime favorite authors are also back. Julianna Morris brings us *The Right Twin for Him* (SR #1676) and Doreen Roberts delivers *One Bride: Baby Included* (SR #1673). And we've got two authors new to the line—one of whom is new to writing! RITA® Award-winning author Angie Ray's newest book, *You're Marrying Her?*, is a fast-paced funny story about a woman who doesn't like her best friend's fiancée. And Patricia Mae White's first novel is about a guy who wants a little help in appealing to the right woman. Here *Practice Makes Mr. Perfect* (SR #1677).

All the best,

Mary-Theresa Hussey

Mary-Theresa Hussey
Senior Editor

Please address questions and book requests to:
Silhouette Reader Service
U.S.: 3010 Walden Ave., P.O. Box 1325, Buffalo, NY 14269
Canadian: P.O. Box 609, Fort Erie, Ont. L2A 5X3

To Catch a Sheik

TERESA SOUTHWICK

DESERT BRIDES

SILHOUETTE *Romance*®

Published by Silhouette Books

America's Publisher of Contemporary Romance

To Susan Mallery,
many thanks for your invaluable assistance
and patient encouragement.

 SILHOUETTE BOOKS

ISBN 0-373-19674-1

TO CATCH A SHEIK

Copyright © 2003 by Teresa Ann Southwick

This edition published by arrangement with Harlequin Books S.A.

® and TM are trademarks of Harlequin Books S.A., used under license. Trademarks indicated with ® are registered in the United States Patent and Trademark Office, the Canadian Trade Marks Office and in other countries.

Visit Silhouette at www.eHarlequin.com

Printed in U.S.A.

Books by Teresa Southwick

Silhouette Romance

Wedding Rings and Baby Things #1209
The Bachelor's Baby #1233
*A Vow, a Ring, a Baby Swing #1349
The Way to a Cowboy's Heart #1383
*And Then He Kissed Me #1405
*With a Little T.L.C. #1421
The Acquired Bride #1474
*Secret Ingredient: Love #1495
*The Last Marchetti Bachelor #1513
**Crazy for Lovin' You #1529
**This Kiss #1541
**If You Don't Know by Now #1560
**What If We Fall in Love? #1572
Sky Full of Promise #1624
†*To Catch a Sheik* #1674

*The Marchetti Family
**Destiny, Texas
†Desert Brides

Silhouette Books

The Fortunes of Texas
Shotgun Vows

Silhouette Special Edition

The Summer House #1510
  "Courting Cassandra"
Midnight, Moonlight
  & Miracles #1517

TERESA SOUTHWICK

lives in Southern California with her hero husband who is more than happy to share with her the male point of view. An avid fan of romance novels, she is delighted to be living out her dream of writing for Silhouette Books.

Teresa has also written historical romances under the same name.

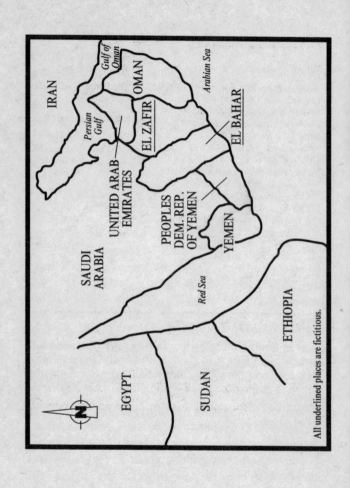

All underlined places are fictitious.

Chapter One

Penelope Colleen Doyle didn't believe in fairy tales. She put no faith in the idea that kissing a frog would create a handsome prince. In fact, the only guys she kissed stayed frogs—or worse—turned into toads. But walking through the royal palace of El Zafir certainly made her *want* to believe.

"Are we almost there?"

She posed the question to her dark-eyed, olive-skinned guide.

"Yes, miss," he said in a softly accented voice. He glanced over his shoulder. "We are nearly there."

She'd forgotten his name. Normally, she had an excellent memory, but nothing about this situation was normal. This was El Zafir—the land of magic, enchantment and romance. She was in the royal palace, with perfectly shined marble hallways, graceful arched doorways and rooms filled with priceless furnishings. But as she put one sensible, low-heeled shoe in front of the other, she had the most absurd desire to leave a trail of cracker crumbs. Just in case she needed to retrace her steps through the maze that was the royal palace.

It was the royal palace, for goodness' sake! But even the panic-induced adrenaline rush produced by that thought couldn't pick up the slack when a body hadn't slept in over twenty-four hours. Crossing numerous time zones tended to take the starch out of a girl. At this moment, she felt as if she'd walked every step of the way from the U.S. of A.

They rounded a corner and stopped before impressive mahogany double doors. The ceiling was so high, the awesome barrier reminded her of a scene from the King Kong movie where the humongous gates were supposed to keep out the giant ape. She was no ape and at five feet one and a half inches, certainly no giant.

"This is the business wing of the palace," her guide explained.

"Is there a map I could use to get my bearings?" she asked. "Something with an *X* that says you are here and a general layout of the rest of the palace?"

"No, miss."

The man didn't crack a smile, not even the barest flicker. If no one in this small but up-and-coming, oil-rich country had a sense of humor, it was going to be a long two years.

He pushed open the right door, revealing a carpeted hall forming a T at the end. Berber carpet if her limited knowledge of fine furnishings could be trusted.

"Follow me, miss."

"Okay."

Like it would occur to her to strike out on her own. She could be lost for days. They'd have to send a search party to look for her. Was there search and rescue in El Zafir?

Her guide walked past several doors, then turned to his right and went through an open door into an office. The room was bigger than her apartment back home. Granted, her apartment was small. But this was awfully Texas-sized for an office.

He held out his hand, indicating the leather love seat against the wall. ''Sit. You'll receive instruction regarding your duties presently.''

''From Princess Farrah Hassan?''

''No.''

Then from whom, she wanted to ask, looking around for a clue. She wouldn't have to guess if the doors had nameplates. You'd think a wealthy nation could find a couple bucks for that.

Without further explanation, her guide turned and left the room. She looked around again, and her jangled nerves kicked up quite a ruckus. Apparently the butterflies in her stomach didn't need it, but the rest of her could certainly use a blast of caffeine.

She didn't see coffee but everything else about the place was pretty darned intimidating. In front of her stood a U-shaped cherry-wood desk, polished to such a shine she could use it for a mirror to do her hair. Although twisting her waist-length hair into a knot at the back of her head was a simple matter and didn't require visual aids. The desk held a computer with printer, scanner and fax machine. Behind it, next to the wall, was a copier. She wondered if all the offices were as well equipped. Or did everyone in the business wing use these machines? If this was the tech center, it made sense that this was where her job orientation would take place.

Then she noticed a closed door to her right. Maybe there was coffee behind it. She could knock and poke her head in to ask. Nope. She'd been ordered to wait and wait she would. With a weary sigh, she sat on the love seat. A second later she sighed for a very different reason. Never in her life had she felt such supple softness. Who knew leather wasn't cold and could feel so fabulously luxurious? She settled in to wait for orders and struggled to keep her eyes open.

Rafiq Hassan, Prince of El Zafir, Minister of Domestic and Foreign Affairs, opened his office door to confer with his secretary. The empty desk reminded him he had no secretary. First thing that morning the efficient young man had been appropriated by his father, King Gamil. His aunt Farrah had promised to send a replacement. Glancing to his left, he saw a young woman sitting on the couch. Sitting was too active a word. Slumped would be more to the point. Was this his substitute?

He walked over and looked down at her. She was dressed in a shapeless khaki dress that covered her from the neck to below her knees, leaving visible her very shapely ankles. Low-heeled shoes covered her feet. She could have been a child except that there was the suggestion of a bosom filling out the bodice of the unflattering garment. She was quite small, he noticed. Unfortunately, the ugly, black-rimmed glasses on her oval face were not.

At the moment she didn't need the spectacles, because her eyes were closed. He was reminded of the American story, the one of Goldilocks that he'd read to his niece and nephew. Her hair *was* golden, and she was sound asleep. Did that make him one of the three bears? His two brothers, Fariq and Kamal, would no doubt be less than flattered at being compared to American bears. Besides, Rafiq had been told he was the family charmer. How bearish could he be?

He bent at the waist and said, "Excuse me?"

Long, lush lashes fluttered. Did they look long and lush because the ugly glasses magnified them? Did objects behind the thick lenses appear larger? When she lifted her eyelids, he wondered that again as very big blue eyes were revealed.

"Hmm?"

"Miss?"

"Hi." She blinked several times and sat up straight, looking around as if she were disoriented. Then she met his gaze. "Guess I'm not in Kansas anymore."

"True."

Before she covered her yawn with a delicate hand, he noted that her teeth were straight and white.

"It's an American expression from the movie *The Wizard of Oz*—when Dorothy realizes that she's very far from home."

"I'm aware of it." He knew the story—the quest of the characters to find home, brain, courage and heart. The last he could relate to very well. "So you're American?" he asked, a purely rhetorical question since her accent clearly placed her.

"Yes," she said. "Just off the plane from Texas."

"I have heard of it."

She smiled. "I'd be surprised if you hadn't. You work here, too?"

"Yes."

"This must be one busy office if there's enough work for two assistants."

Assistant? She thought he was an assistant? He

opened his mouth to set her straight when she slid to the edge of the love seat and stretched, arching her back so that her suggestion of a bosom became rounded breasts straining against the buttons of her dress. No thick magnifying lenses there, and the objects were most impressive.

"Could you point me in the direction of the coffee-pot?" she asked.

"I can ring for some," he said absently, his gaze preoccupied.

"That would be great. I'll be forever in your debt."

Rafiq went to the desk and picked up the phone. "Coffee, please. Very strong."

"Bless you."

When he looked at her again, she was peering intently at him through the hideous lenses of her glasses, not unlike the way he'd been looking upon her.

"What is it?" he asked.

"I'm sorry. I didn't mean to stare. It's just—"

"Tell me."

"No." She shook her head. "You'll think I'm weird. If we're going to be working together, weird isn't exactly the best foot to put forward."

"I promise not to think that." Now he was curious. "Why did you have that look on your face? Do I have a wart on my nose? A smudge on my face? You find me strange looking?"

"Oh, no. You're very handsome." She ducked her head, obviously flustered. "I mean if the rest of the men in this country are anything like you—" Her cheeks flushed a delightful pink. "I'm sorry. I hope you don't mind my saying that. It's just— I had no idea. In my research on El Zafir, I didn't see anything about— I'm sorry. But you did ask."

"Yes, I did." Her flustered manner told him she hadn't planned to say that. The compliment was honest, ingenuous and charmingly innocent. He very nearly forgave her for mistaking him for an assistant.

"Where I come from, cowboys are the masculine standard. Most women wouldn't think of office staff as macho. But most women haven't been to El Zafir."

He couldn't decide whether to be flattered or insulted and made a mental note to make discreet inquiries about Texas cowboys. He also revoked his momentary weakness regarding forgiveness. But strangely enough, he wanted her to go on. "So you're an assistant?"

She nodded, then took off her glasses and rubbed her eyes. He expected to see black makeup, mascara or raccoon eyes as women had told him it was called when it ran. But, there was none. She wore no cosmetics. Still, her skin was flawless—smooth and quite soft-looking.

"I just arrived in El Zafir this morning," she explained. "I was supposed to be here two days ago, but flights out of North Texas were delayed because of storms. Where I come from they say if you don't like the weather, just wait a minute. But this time I wasn't that lucky."

"So how did you come to my—to El Zafir, Miss—"

"Doyle. Penelope Colleen Doyle. It rhymes with oil."

"Yes."

"You can call me Penny."

"Penny," he said, testing the name given to the lowest valued coin in U.S. currency.

"I was hired by Princess Farrah Hassan. Have you met her?"

His lips twitched, but he held back the threatening smile. "Once or twice."

"She's pretty impressive. A real force of nature. The king's sister. I'm to be her assistant."

"When did this happen?"

"A month ago."

"And you've just arrived today?"

She nodded. "I had to settle the lease on my apartment and arrange storage for my things."

She looked very young to have the responsibility of living on her own. "How old are you?" he couldn't help asking.

One blond eyebrow lifted questioningly. "In the States if you ask that question, you're likely to get decked. It's not considered politically correct to inquire about a woman's age."

"I know politics." And women, he added silently. "You look too young to be—"

"I'm twenty-two." She sat up straighter. "Not that it's your concern, but I have a degree in early childhood education as well as business. I had a double major in college. I needed a job. With a good salary. So I submitted my résumé with an exclusive agency that handles child care for wealthy families. After looking at qualifications and pictures, the princess picked me, among others. According to the agency director, she was looking for a plain nanny."

"Is that so?"

"I didn't think it was appropriate to ask. But why do you suppose the princess was specifically looking for someone plain?"

There was no reason to reveal that he was responsible for the stipulation. "I can't say."

She shrugged. "Me, neither. But I was confident that I fit the qualifications and was just what they were looking for."

"I see." He might be the family charmer, but her straightforward declaration left him at a loss. His knowledge of women was based on the tall, sophisticated, glamorous type. Not small women with big, unattractive glasses.

"I prefer to meet life head-on. If you bury your head in the sand, you leave your—" She stopped and pushed her glasses up more securely on her nose. "Well, the rest of yourself exposed. If you know what I mean. I'm nothing if not practical. It's best to face facts and not expect the fairy tale. Don't you agree?"

He wasn't sure how to answer. Best to go in a different direction. "So you got an interview with my— with the princess?"

"Yes. I received a round-trip plane ticket to New York. It was my first time on an airplane. Very exciting. But there was a problem."

"Is that so?"

The office doors opened and a female servant wheeled in a cart bearing a silver service and china cups. "Thank you, Salima."

"You're welcome, Your—"

"Leave it by the desk," he said, quickly interrupting her. "I'll take care of it."

"Very well." She bowed slightly and backed out of the room.

Wide-eyed, Penny watched her. "Wow. Is everyone so deferential? We in the States could take lessons. You're going to have to help me. I wouldn't want to

offend anyone. If you see me doing anything disre-
spectful, please take me aside so I don't make a fool
of myself.''

"You're an American," he said as if that was answer enough. Then he picked up the coffeepot and
aimed the silver spout at one of the delicate china
cups.

"Would you mind pouring me some, too? I can't
believe I fell asleep. Now I need to kick-start my mo-
tor.''

"All evidence to the contrary.''

"Am I talking too much?" She went on without
waiting for an answer. "I do that sometimes. But today it's worse than usual. Probably because I'm tired
and nervous. A bad combination. Does it bother you?
The princess didn't seem to mind.''

"She is a very strong woman. Cream or sugar?''

"Black is fine," she said.

He handed her the cup. "You were saying?''

"Where was I?" She took a sip and thought for a
moment. "Oh, yes. I was in New York to meet the
princess. Wouldn't you know it? My flight was delayed.''

"North Texas weather?''

She nodded. "You really listen, don't you? Then
there was traffic getting through the city. By the time
I got to her suite in the hotel, which was pretty hoity-
toity I can tell you, she had already hired someone
else.''

"A plain nanny?''

"Yes." She frowned. "I still can't imagine why
that would be a criteria for employment. Go figure.''

"Indeed.''

"Anyway, the princess was so nice and easy to be

with. She invited me to stay for lunch. We did the girl-talk thing and bonded over chocolate.''

"Bonded?"

"You know. Where women share stories that bring them closer together?"

"Ah. Chocolate, you say?"

She nodded. "Godiva, I think. Very yummy. Anyway, she said she liked me and she was in need of an assistant. So she hired me. She made me an offer I couldn't refuse. But then you already know how well a job in the palace of the royal family of El Zafir pays."

"I do indeed," he agreed.

"Room and board is included."

"Truly a fine offer."

"You can say that again— What did you say your name was?" she asked, then took another sip of coffee. "How rude of me to forget. I can only plead fatigue. After a good night's sleep, I'll be back in fighting form. I'm usually very good with names."

"I don't believe I mentioned it."

He found her intriguing. For a woman pleading weariness, she had an amazing amount of energy. With proper rest she would no doubt be a, what was that American expression? Ball of fire? Yes. That was definitely Penny. He couldn't help wondering if her dynamic verve was reserved strictly for work. Or if it spilled over to the personal—to the man in her life.

"You're staring at me with the oddest expression. Do I have a smudge on my face? A wart on my nose? Do you find me strange looking?" she teased.

"Not at all."

"Surely your name can't be that bad. Since we're

going to work together, it might be a good idea to tell me so I don't have to call 'hey you.'"

He straightened to his full six-foot-two-inch height. "I am Rafiq Hassan, Prince of El Zafir, Minister of Domestic and Foreign Affairs."

Her eyes grew round as the china cup fell from her hands, hit her knees, then the floor, splattering the coffee that hadn't stained her dress on the light-colored Berber carpet.

Her mouth opened, but no words came out. A victory indeed. He'd finally rendered her speechless.

Rafiq knocked on the door to his aunt Farrah's suite of rooms in the wing of the palace where the royal family resided. At her muffled "Come in," he entered. His footsteps echoed on the marble tiles of the foyer as he walked into the living room with floor-to-ceiling windows overlooking the Arabian Sea. A large semicircular white sofa on the plush light-colored carpet dominated the center of the room. The only splash of color in the suite came from expensive original paintings hanging on the walls. His father's sister owned a world-famous art collection.

He stood by the sofa and looked down at her, with papers in her lap and spread around her. "I would like to speak with you, Aunt Farrah."

"Of course. What is it, Rafiq?"

"In a word—Penny."

She smiled, and the years melted away. His aunt, in her fifties, was still an attractive and vibrant woman. Her dark hair was cut in a sleek style that brushed the collar of her tailored turquoise Chanel suit.

"She is wonderful, no?"

"She is—something."

"Why? What is wrong?" she asked, frowning. She set aside her work.

"She fell asleep on the couch in my office."

"Poor thing. In her defense I have to say it's quite a comfortable couch." She clucked sympathetically. "A grueling trip. I was told the dear child insisted on beginning work as agreed. Wouldn't hear of postponing her start even for a day."

"I want her beheaded."

"Certainly a fitting reward for her dedication."

"I'm joking."

"I'm glad to hear it." Farrah laughed. "The government outlawed that form of punishment many years ago, even before I was born."

"Cutting out her tongue would be more appropriate, I think." He paced in front of her. "Yes. Excellent idea if I do say so myself. Make the consequences fit the crime."

"My dear nephew, what crime has she committed?"

"She is—" He stopped, unable to find the words to describe his feelings. "A woman."

"Ah," his aunt said, as if that explained everything. "You are bemused by her."

"Certainly not. I've never met a woman I couldn't understand." The lie was a very small one. He *hadn't* ever met a woman he couldn't understand. Until today.

"So you're intrigued."

"Nonsense." He shook his head and turned away, staring out the French doors to her balcony that looked out over the ocean. "Completely, utterly absurd."

"Rafiq, have you ever been in love?"

He didn't know how to answer the question. Many

women had charmed him. Certainly infatuation had been involved, but love?

"Don't start with me, Aunt. Love is a luxury not permitted a prince of the royal blood. It's all about duty. I will marry and produce heirs."

"When?"

"When I am ready." Glancing over his shoulder, he said, "But I fail to see what this has to do with Penny Doyle."

Farrah clasped her hands together in her lap. "Because of your mother's tragic premature death, I can't help feeling as if your education in this regard has been sadly neglected. Servants, tutors, boarding school…"

"I had an excellent education. Now, about this small American—"

"Penny. I found her a breath of fresh air. But it's just as well you don't agree."

He turned and steeled himself against the knowing expression on his aunt's face. He reminded himself that she was a woman, his elder, a cherished family member and deserving of his respect, honor and protection. But the gleam in her eyes made him wonder if he might not be the one in need of protection.

"Why would I agree? She's a small, insignificant young woman from Texas." He walked to the French doors and stood with his hands clasped behind his back. "It was my understanding that things from Texas were much larger."

"Yes. Penny is the exception, I assume."

"Penny. Even her name is trifling."

"Have you ever heard the expression 'find a penny, pick it up, all day long you'll have good luck'?"

"Perhaps. Penny Doyle—rhymes with oil," he

murmured, unable to stop his mouth from curving up at the memory of her words. He was glad his back was to his keen-eyed aunt so that she didn't see.

Behind him she coughed. He turned and noticed the glitter of amusement in her black eyes. "Are you all right?" he asked. If he didn't know better, he'd think she was laughing at him.

"I'm absolutely marvelous."

"And why is that?"

"Your reaction to Penny is just what I'd hoped. Now, I don't have to warn you to keep your distance."

"If you're concerned about it, Aunt, then why did Father take my own assistant and give me a woman?"

She shifted slightly. In anyone less regal, it would have been a squirm. "He needed someone experienced. And he is the king. Penny is perfect for your…needs. Business needs," she added. "If I were you, I would think twice before questioning your father."

"All right then. But I'm wounded that you feel it's necessary to question my behavior."

"Aside from your reputation as a bit of a rogue with women, I'm concerned about Penny."

"Why? She could talk the ears off an elephant," he pointed out.

"She was badly used by a man."

Rafiq frowned. Penny was vexing, but in an impish sort of way. "How?"

"She told me the whole horrid story in New York. Her mother died when Penny was twelve or thirteen. The woman was single, a teacher. Yet she managed to leave her daughter an inheritance that was put into trust. The dear child planned to open a preschool until that unprincipled scoundrel romanced her in order to abscond with her money. She's unlikely to trust a man ever again,'' she finished.

"He is not a man. A man would not treat a woman so. Especially a woman like—"

"Like what?'' his aunt asked, one eyebrow lifted.

"Never mind. I would like to meet this man,'' he said through clenched teeth. "Horsewhipping would be too good for him.''

"I agree.'' She nodded grimly, then the look was gone, replaced by a serene smile. "But Penny is here now and we will take care of her. That is, *I* will look after her. In my opinion, things couldn't be better,'' she said.

"On the contrary.'' When he left the young woman, he was merely bemused by her. After learning her story, he found himself mildly intrigued. It made him a bit uneasy, something he normally didn't feel around women. Without a doubt he could also say he didn't much like the feeling. Perhaps he could change his aunt's mind about assigning to him this particular woman.

"What is it, Rafiq?''

"Things could be much improved if father would return my assistant. Then you could have your Penny Doyle—with my heartfelt approval and best wishes that your sanity and hearing remain undiminished.''

She shook her head. "I'm afraid that returning your assistant won't be possible for some time.''

"Why not?''

"That's up to your father,'' she answered.

"I've taken your advice and thought twice. I will speak to him about the matter.''

"In the meantime, with preparations about to begin for the international charity ball hosted for the first time by El Zafir, you will need help. A woman's touch.''

"You're a woman—and my co-chair for the event,'' he pointed out reasonably. "Isn't that enough?''

"Penny will work with both of us.''

Rafiq didn't like the sound of that. He would try another tack. "Is that fair to her? To work for me as well? By yourself, you are a formidable taskmaster.''

"Not unfairly so. Besides, I suspect Penny is a very hard worker.''

"If she can close her mouth long enough,'' he grumbled.

"I found her charming.''

"Is that her only qualification? It's my understanding she was seeking employment as nanny to Fariq's children.''

"Yes. But she was so…energized and quite bright. She has a degree, a double major—early childhood education and business. Because, she informed me, a preschool is still a business. She has a glowing reference from Sam Prescott.''

Sam Prescott was from a wealthy Texas family. He'd been Rafiq's friend since they were boys. Over the years they'd joked that if America had royalty, Sam and his brothers would be their sheiks. Their fathers knew each other well, in addition to sharing business interests.

"How does Sam know her?'' he asked.

"Prescott International bestows grants to needy, gifted students. Penny was chosen as the recipient, and the family took a personal interest in her education and career. She was in the top of her business classes and earned an internship at Prescott corporate headquarters in Dallas. So I have it on good authority that she's quick, intelligent, hardworking and more than capable of being trained.''

''Apparently, that will be my responsibility.'' He glared at his aunt, but she didn't refute his words.

''Such a look would frighten small children. Tell me you didn't look at her that way, Rafiq?'' Her expressive eyes opened wide. ''You're the diplomat of the family. If you—''

''I'm not in the habit of frightening small children or women. But there is the matter of the coffee—''

It had practically taken an act of God to render her speechless. Fortunately, the liquid had cooled and she wasn't hurt. He felt the slightest twinge of conscience at his part in the incident.

''What about the coffee?'' she asked.

''It fell from her hands.''

''Did you do something to make it fall?''

''I merely introduced myself.''

After letting her believe he was an assistant. And coaxing her into revealing that she thought he was very handsome. Actually, he'd found the disguise liberating. He doubted she would have spoken so freely if he hadn't let her assume he was an ordinary man. He was accustomed to flattery from women, but because Penny hadn't known his true identity, her compliment was rooted in sincerity.

''Where is she now?'' his aunt inquired, frowning.

''In her room, the one you assigned her here in the guest quarters of the palace. I advised her to take the rest of the day off to recover from her journey.''

She nodded approvingly. ''Good. And I'm pleased we have talked. So that I can remind you one last time, Rafiq. You are not to be charming to Penny. Just until other arrangements can be made, she is your assistant and is to be nothing more,'' she added. ''We cannot have the business of El Zafir disrupted because you've charmed yet another female member of the staff.''

''Thank you, Aunt Farrah,'' he said, unable to suppress a smile.

''That was not meant to be a compliment. I'm going to say this one more time. Do nothing out of the ordinary. Do not go out of your way to be nice to Penny. Simple courtesy in the work environment. That is all.''

He pulled himself up to his full height. ''I am a prince of the royal blood. Benevolence is my responsibility. You yourself instructed me in the necessity of being gracious. I find no reason to apologize for so thoroughly learning the lesson you set before me.''

''I also taught you to respect your elders.'' She sniffed. ''You're acting like a strong-willed little boy.''

''On the contrary,'' he said. ''I don't see that at all.''

''Of course not. You never do. Or your brothers, either.''

''What do Kamal and Fariq have to do with anything?'' he asked.

''The crown prince and minister of oil respectively have nothing whatever to do with our conversation. I was merely stating a fact.''

''The men of the royal family of Hassan have sworn allegiance to country and family,'' he said. ''We are the protectors of the people of El Zafir. We can't afford to be wrong.''

''It is a sacred and awesome responsibility,'' she agreed. ''And I have found a young woman who, I believe, will make an excellent assistant. Someone bright and entertaining who I would like to remain in my employ for a long time to come. I am merely requesting that you do nothing to facilitate her return to the United States.''

''I wouldn't think of it.''

She frowned at him. ''It makes me nervous when you are so agreeable.'' He opened his mouth to protest, but she waved him away. ''Go tell the king or one of your brothers. They might believe your denials.''

''I am not as agreeable as you might think.'' For some reason, he felt compelled to defend himself. Yet it hadn't come out right at all.

''For the sake of palace peace, I hope so.''

Suppressing a long-suffering sigh, he bowed slightly in deference to her age and family position.

As he left Farrah's rooms, his thoughts turned to the young American. Bright and entertaining? He wasn't certain he'd seen that side of Penny Doyle. Perhaps he should talk with her again. Merely to ascertain whether or not he'd underestimated his new assistant. If for no other reason than to get to know her better.

So the business of El Zafir would run smoothly.

Chapter Two

Penny paced back and forth in front of the French doors in her room. Wired by nerves and the small amount of caffeine consumed before the disaster, she couldn't relax. It was a good thing the suite was so large—lots of space to pace in. If only she could sleep. Oblivion would be preferable to the mental kicking her backside was taking. She alternated between how could she have been so stupid and how could he have let her go on?

Rafiq. A rakish name. It suited him. He was very good-looking. But that didn't excuse his behavior. He was a prince, a ruler of his country. *That* excused his behavior. Mortified, she remembered the conversation—her inane prattle. He knew how well a staff member in the royal palace was paid. He'd seen Princess Farrah once or twice. She'd told him he was handsome, for goodness' sake. But that information he'd pried out of her.

She covered her face with her hands, wishing fatigue could block out the humiliating scene. What a fool she'd made of herself. And he'd let her even after she'd asked him to help her not to do that!

It wasn't the first time a man had made a fool of her. Last time, the man had taken her money and disappeared. This time, *she'd* been told to disappear. His exact words—she should take the rest of the day off. To acclimate. Was that El Zafirian for get ready to be drawn and quartered at dawn for the crime of impertinence?

"I almost wish I was dead," she said to the white walls surrounding her. "But I'd prefer something nonviolent and less messy."

She had to admit that if she breathed her last at dawn, these digs were a fabulous place to spend her final hours. The walls were white, the starkness broken by colorful tapestries hanging in the living room, dining area and bedroom. A low, soft sofa took up one corner of the room that faced a lush, colorful garden. Flowers and greenery abounded below her window. She couldn't see the ocean, but on the balcony she'd breathed in the fragrance of sea air mixed with the perfume of the flowers. The two blended, creating an intoxicating scent she'd never before experienced.

The bedroom contained a large four-poster bed, matching dresser and armoire—as if she had enough clothes to fill the two pieces of furniture. In the corner was a chair and ottoman covered in white cashmere, or so she'd been told by the maid who'd helped her unpack her meager belongings. What was she doing here? It was a rhetorical question, which fortunately didn't require an answer. She wouldn't be around long enough to bother with one. Not after what she'd done—correction—not after she'd been baited and reeled in.

Then the baiter in question—one Rafiq Hassan, Prince of El Zafir—had calmly given her the day off. Wouldn't it have been simpler to just send her to the airport? Surely he wouldn't allow her to stay after she'd insulted him.

It didn't matter that there were no nameplates in his office. That should have been a dead giveaway. Although, she wasn't especially comfortable with the dead part. Everyone knew the royal family. Why would they need their names on the doors? Lack of sleep could no longer be an excuse for what she'd done. Hands down, she would win ninny of the year or the El Zafirian equivalent. Being new to the country should be considered mitigating circumstances. And he—Rafiq—had set her up. But he was a prince; she was a pauper.

An unexpected knock on the door made her jump. Her heart contracted painfully. Here it comes, she thought. We who are about to die, or be ignominiously deported back to the U.S., salute you.

She opened the door. It was *him!* For the second time that day she found herself in the unnatural condition of being unable to form words.

"May I come in?" he asked.

"Of course." She pulled the door wide and stood back, allowing him entrance. After all, this was his place. Place? Oops. Palace. Far different from the average, ordinary, run-of-the-mill man's place.

He looked at her. "You've changed."

"Not really. I'm the same person I was a while ago. I just don't have the words—"

He pointed to her pants. "I meant your clothes."

"Oh." She followed his glance to her bare feet, jeans and Don't Mess With Texas T-shirt. When she met his gaze again, she thought it contained a spark of—something she didn't understand. But she could only think of one word to describe his black eyes. Smoldering.

Her research on the country in general and the royal family in particular had revealed that his last name, Hassan, meant handsome and he certainly lived up to it. His thick black hair was cut short. Subtle waving told her that if it was longer, some serious curling would happen. His face was a composition of high cheekbones, straight nose and square jaw that came dangerously close to male perfection. Broad shoulders and a wide chest fit his tall body. His sinfully expensive navy-blue business suit highlighted lean, masculine strength. Then she remembered her tasteless remark about cowboys being the standard of male appeal in Texas. Prince Rafiq Hassan had just upped the benchmark. She had the heart palpitations, weak knees and sweaty palms to prove it.

"I don't—"

"Yes?" he prompted.

"What do I call you?" she blurted out. "Your Majesty? Your Highness? Your Worship? The member of the royal family formerly and still known as Prince?"

She was being impertinent, but she couldn't help it. That's who she was. Besides, what did she have to lose? She'd already put her foot in her mouth. Even though he should share part of the blame for leading her on, he was probably there to tell her she was fired. From here she had nowhere to go but the airport.

"You may call me Your Highness, Prince Rafiq

Hassan, Minister of Foreign and Domestic Affairs, the bountiful and benevolent.''

She felt like reaching for her scratch pad to write down the lengthy form of address when she noticed that his wonderful firm lips were curving up at the corners. ''You're joking,'' she accused.

''Yes.''

''Oh, thank goodness.''

''What?''

''You *do* have a sense of humor.''

''Of course. Why would you doubt it?'' He shrugged and extended one hand in a self-effacing gesture.

There was a Band-Aid on his index finger, sporting a cartoon character. It was a sign. He was more than a pompous, arrogant baiter of unsuspecting women.

''At our first meeting you never cracked a smile,'' she reminded him.

''That is why I'm here.''

''To show me you can smile?''

''No. To…start again.''

For half a second, she'd thought he was going to apologize for leading her on, making her appear foolish.

She looked up at him, way up, then adjusted her glasses more securely on her nose. ''I figured you were here to can me.''

''Excuse me?''

''You know, terminate me.'' She shook her head. ''Bad choice of words.''

''Why?''

''I was wondering if I'd be drawn and quartered in the city square at dawn.''

''Actually, the idea of beheading came up.''

She gasped. "No!"

"Yes. Then the merits of cutting out your tongue."

She backed up a step before noticing his smile. A full-on, showing-his-great-teeth, go-for-broke, steal-her-heart grin. "You're teasing me."

"Yes." He slid his hands into the pockets of his slacks, upsetting the sleek line at the bottom of the matching jacket. "By 'can' and 'terminate' you meant revoke your employment."

"Right. Fire me." Although the way he looked could give a whole new meaning to the word. He was what the girls back home called a "hottie."

"I'm not here to do that."

"Well, that's a relief. Although you must admit that if you'd told me right away who you are, there wouldn't be a large coffee stain on the carpet in your office."

"I don't have to admit anything," he said. "I am the prince."

"Of course." And exactly the reason she decided against taking him to task for leading her on. Besides, it looked as if she was getting a reprieve. Bearding the lion in his den, so to speak, probably wasn't the wisest course. "And a prince is the master of all he surveys."

"Something like that," he said, a sparkle in his eyes betraying that he was amused.

"If you're not here to admit anything, then why are you here?"

"To welcome you—properly—to El Zafir."

"Thank you—" She tipped her head to the side and said, "You still haven't told me what to call you."

"Prince Rafiq in public. In private, when we are working, my given name is appropriate."

Rafiq. The name raised shivers on her arms that

scurried over her chest and abdomen. He wasn't like anyone she'd ever met. Just his name conjured up visions of mystery and magic, enchantment and romance. For the first time, she believed what the travel posters had claimed about his country.

"Prince Rafiq," she said, testing the name.

"Since it has fallen to me to train you—"

"But I'm supposed to work for Princess Farrah."

"There's been a change of plan. My father has appropriated my secretary and my aunt—"

"Princess Farrah?"

He nodded. "My father's sister. She has given you to me."

The shivers, which had barely disappeared, kicked up again at the suggestion that she'd been given to him. Lordy, why did her mind have to go there? It wasn't really such a stretch. This was an exotic country with a different history and culture. Myths of women being swept off their feet and literally carried away by mesmerizing men had been widely romanticized in movies and books. Feminists might object, but Penny had the feeling if any of them took one look at Rafiq, bras would go up in flames and not because anyone was protesting.

"So I'm to work with you?"

He nodded. "If you wish I can arrange for chocolate to be brought. We can do the bonding thing."

"You really are different from other men," she blurted out.

Good Lord! She couldn't believe she'd said that. It was completely inappropriate. Granted she'd said something similar when she'd thought he was an assistant like herself. But now she knew who he was. Besides that, it was flirtatious. She'd never been a flirt.

Partly because she'd never had the time. Partly because her nature didn't lean toward flirting. But her remark had come dangerously close. Was it something in the air of exotic El Zafir? Something in the water? Or was it a mysterious something in the man that unleashed her inner flirt?

"Different?" he asked. He didn't look shocked or offended, merely curious.

"Where I come from, there are talk shows dedicated to the fact that most men don't listen, let alone remember," she explained.

"Perhaps cowboys leave something to be desired as the masculine standard in your country?"

He really *had* listened, she thought, as heat surged into her cheeks. "Maybe listening and remembering are highly overrated skills."

He smiled. Were his teeth really white enough to be featured in an ad for dental bleaching? Or did they just look that way because his skin was so very tanned?

"With all due respect," he said, "I have yet to meet a woman who prefers a man to ignore her."

She couldn't help wondering how much research he'd done on women. Quite a bit according to what she'd read about the royal family. She'd seen articles in the tabloids detailing the romantic exploits of Prince Rafiq. She'd even seen his picture, which made her feel all the more ridiculous for not recognizing him. But in person, the flesh-and-blood hunk bore no resemblance to the one-dimensional Don Juan she'd seen in the papers.

How many women had he been involved with? Ten? Twenty? A hundred? And how many cowboys had she been with? Zero. Zilch. Nada. So who was better qualified to judge?

"Okay. You get points for listening and remembering," she agreed.

"Thank you." He looked around her suite. "I trust the accommodations are satisfactory?"

"Oh, yes." She followed his gaze. "This is the most beautiful place I've ever seen."

"As compared to Texas?"

"As compared to anywhere. Even the hotel where I met your aunt."

"It is more spartan than the New York hotel she prefers."

Penny nodded. "But there's something to be said for simplicity. Sometimes less is more."

"I know precisely what you mean." He met her gaze and his own darkened. His irises were blacker than midnight—smoldering.

There was that word again. It took the air from her lungs. But didn't fire do that, steal oxygen? Where was an extinguisher when you really needed one?

"Tell me about yourself, Penny."

The question surprised her. She wasn't sure why, except that it seemed odd for a member of the ruling family to care about someone like her. The hired help. Then she remembered the cartoon Band-Aid. He must have interacted with his brother's children and forgotten it was on his finger. She took courage from that. He was a flesh-and-blood man who put his pants on one leg at a time.

Speaking of legs, he'd been standing for a really long time. "Would you like to sit down?"

He only hesitated a moment before saying, "Yes.

Thank you.'' With athletic, catlike grace he sat on the sofa then indicated the space beside him. "Please."

She did as he requested, but left an appropriate distance between them. "So what would you like to know about me?"

"Why did you leave your country and take a job halfway around the world in El Zafir?"

There were so many reasons. "Your country is very progressive."

He nodded. "We're working hard to make it so. What else?"

It was as if he could read her mind. "I believe we've already established that a position in the palace pays well," she said, smiling.

He grinned in return. "Yes, I believe we did. Is money important to you?"

"Only someone who's never needed it would ask that question."

"Is that a yes?" He lifted one dark eyebrow.

"It is."

"Tell me why."

"You don't really want to know."

"On the contrary."

"Money is important to me because my mother worked very hard for it."

"Your father?"

"I never knew him. It was always only my mother and me. She died when I was young."

He looked very grave. "Mine did as well. Aunt Farrah filled the void when my mother was gone."

"You're lucky. I didn't have anyone to fill the emptiness. The small nest egg she managed to leave me didn't take away the pain when she was gone. I was raised in an orphanage."

"I see."

She found his matter-of-fact response strangely appropriate. "I'm sorry" was a meaningless, conditioned response and brought little comfort. "At eighteen, the state says you're an adult and on your own."

"The state is wrong," he answered. "Such an age is still a child."

She shrugged. "Maybe. But I was determined to get a degree."

"And you did—in early childhood education and business. My aunt tells me you interned for Sam Prescott in Dallas."

"Yes. The Prescotts have been very good to me. In fact Sam is the one who suggested I might think about working in El Zafir."

Because she'd planned to start her own preschool. And she'd foolishly given away her seed money. But as comfortable as Rafiq made her feel, she still didn't think he would want to hear about all that. Or maybe it was more that she didn't want to confess how stupid she'd been. Taken in by a handsome man. She'd vowed never again to be suckered by a good-looking game player.

He was staring at her and the intensity of his gaze made her wonder if he could see all the way to her soul. She hoped not. He wouldn't want someone so gullible working for him.

"I have known Sam Prescott since we were boys. Is there a particular reason that earning a lot of money is important to you?" he asked.

Because a promise was a promise. The vow she'd made a long time ago meant everything to her. But he wouldn't want to hear about that. He was a businessman. "It's my dream to open a preschool, possibly in

a corporate environment. That way it could be subsi-
dized by the company.''

"Why?''

"As a businessman yourself, I should think that
would be obvious. Corporate sponsorship would in-
crease the success ratio—''

"No. I meant why a preschool?''

"Oh. Well. I like children.'' She met his gaze and
was surprised he didn't look bored. In fact, he gave a
good imitation of being interested, which gave her the
courage to continue. "I think that's hereditary. My
mother loved teaching elementary school. Before I
was old enough to go to school, she struggled with
the cost of child care. She always said a mother
shouldn't have to choose between a safe place for her
child at the expense of a stimulating environment.''

"A preschool would do both?''

"Yes. As long as women are part of the workforce,
and I don't see that changing anytime soon, quality
care for children will be an issue.''

"In my country as well.''

"Really?''

Rafiq watched as she made herself comfortable on
the sofa. She scooted back and, though it was low, her
short legs didn't allow her feet to touch. Small feet,
he noted and bare so he could see her red-painted toe-
nails. Strangely unexpected—and appealing. She
tucked her legs to the side and rested her elbow on
the back of the furniture. Her golden hair was no
longer pulled severely back from her oval face and
secured in a bun at her nape. The waist-length strands
cascaded around her like a silky sunshine curtain, beg-
ging a man to run his fingers through it.

He'd struggled with his reaction to her ever since

she'd opened the door to him. Oddly enough, the shapeless khaki dress she'd worn earlier had been distraction enough. But jeans outlined her small waist and slender legs. As body types went, she was the complete opposite of the women who caught his eye. Speaking of eyes, hers regarded him through huge glasses. Obviously, she expected him to continue the conversation. And he would. As soon as he remembered what they'd been discussing.

"I didn't think many women worked outside the home in El Zafir," she said.

Ah, he thought. Preschools. "More and more educated women are choosing careers in this country. We've overlooked this great natural resource and vital addition to our workforce far too long."

"Then child care becomes a problem."

"Exactly."

"I would still like to know why your brother specifically requested a homely nanny for his children."

How could he get her to forget that particular question? His gaze settled on her mouth. Earlier, when she'd talked so much, he hadn't noticed how very lush and full her lips were. He had a sudden inclination to taste her. That might make her forget about homely nannies. But he forced the thought away. She was his temporary assistant. Nothing more. And he would do well to remember that and forget how curvy she looked in her jeans.

He was her employer. And she was hardly more than a child. He was twenty-nine years old, but she made him feel ancient.

"I need to go." He stood up. "About work."

"Yes?"

She stood also. So small. Her head barely came to

his shoulder. He felt a sudden strange burst of protectiveness for her. The same as he would feel for a child, he amended. This surprising reaction was merely the result of being with much taller women. None of them had ever evoked this reaction of wanting to stand between her and whatever storms life would blow into her path.

Penny had been hurt. Because his aunt had revealed that to him, he'd recognized the disillusionment in the depths of her eyes when she'd talked about her dream. Rage flared inside him. Again he wanted to make the jackal who had taken advantage of this innocent pay for his unforgivable sin.

"What about work?" she asked.

"Yes, work."

"What time do you want me to report to the office?"

"Nine."

She smiled. "At least there won't be commuter traffic."

"No." He cleared his throat. "About your attire—"

"Your aunt already filled me in on that. No pants in public. She said in this country a woman covers her arms, and skirts must be worn well below the knee."

"Yes."

He should be relieved that she was aware. But he found himself strangely heavyhearted that jeans were inappropriate and Penny was aware of it.

"Tomorrow then," she said.

"Yes. Tomorrow."

"I'm looking forward to it."

As was he. Far more than he should.

Chapter Three

Penny closed the door to her suite and set off to dine with the Hassans. Other than feeling like Dorothy making her way to the Emerald City or a wide-eyed whacked-out character from a fractured fairy tale, she was looking forward to it. Really and truly. Eating with the royal family. Every last one. All in one place. All at the same time.

Yeah. And any minute now she would flap her wings and fly like a fairy godmother.

On the upside, after a week in El Zafir she was a bit more comfortable making her way through the palace without a compass or a clear view of the North Star. No, she knew her way to the royal dining room, and it was all she could do not to take off in the opposite direction. But how far could she get on legs that shook like tree limbs in a hurricane? If the invitation had come from anyone but Princess Farrah...

She would have refused? Yeah, like that was going to happen. Her common sense told her it wasn't smart to bite the hand that feeds you. Retreat was not an option. Besides, she liked and respected the princess.

If only she wasn't so nervous.

Descending the stairway, Penny held the polished mahogany railing. Each marble step had Berber carpet in the center. At the bottom, she walked to her left and pushed open one of the double doors into the dining room. Over and over she repeated to herself, "I will not talk too much."

She poked her head inside to get her bearings before everyone showed up. Her heart nearly stopped as she saw the royal family already there. She quickly counted heads. Yup—all of them. Was she late? She hated being late. She despised walking into a room where everyone could look at her when she arrived. At least no one was sitting at the table yet. Table, ha. It was long—really long. An airport runway—without landing lights and covered by a lovely tablecloth.

Penny shook her wrist, then looked at her watch. She'd given herself enough time to be ten minutes early and catch her breath waiting for everyone else to walk in. But no. Just her luck to dine with the only royal family on the planet more punctual than herself. She loathed lateness. And nerves. It was the reason she'd had such a disastrous first meeting with Rafiq. Nerves and lateness, she had learned the hard way, were a recipe for disaster.

The butterflies in her stomach began a rousing rendition of the cancan as she noted the sheer number of people present. She'd met them all, one at a time. But all this royalty gathered together in one room was enough to give her a case of hives. How did someone like her deal with royals in droves? Very carefully, she thought, stifling a giggle that could turn hysterical at the drop of a hat, crown or, God forbid, coffee cup.

Like a magnet picking up metal, her gaze homed in on her boss. He was talking with his brothers and suddenly smiled. In an instant, the serious, aloof, authoritative man she'd become familiar with disappeared. The expression changed him from handsome to hubba-hubba gorgeous in zero point two seconds. Her legs started shaking again, but for a very different reason. She found she was much more comfortable with her boss, the prince, than this man who smiled or, oddly enough, the one who teased about cutting out her tongue.

Rafiq.

He'd told her to address him by his given name in private. Was there a rule about how many people constituted public? Did it matter that this was his family? Should she call him Prince Rafiq or lose the title? She would seriously consider selling her soul for just a drop of social confidence.

Glancing down, she sighed at her long-sleeved, high-necked black knit dress skimming the tops of her ankles. She recalled the teenaged salesclerk at the store where she'd purchased it telling her you could never go wrong with black. Her first mistake had been believing a teenager with pink hair. Penny had gone so very wrong. But then, she didn't have the budget to go right.

"Ah, Penny." Princess Farrah, in a dark green silk dress with matching heels and diamonds at her ears and neck, came forward to greet her.

"Good evening, Your Highness." Penny looked around. "I hope I'm not late. You said seven—"

"You are perfect, my dear. Isn't she, Gamil?'' she said to the king.

Two steps away, the distinguished ruler turned at her words. He joined them and bowed slightly from the waist. "Miss Doyle. I'm very pleased you could join us for dinner this evening."

"You are most kind to include me.'' She looked around at everyone. The princess had told her it would be an intimate dinner with the family. Meeting the woman's friendly gaze, Penny asked before she could stop herself, "Do you dress like this for dinner every night?"

The princess laughed. "Three or four times a week. The other nights one or more of us has an official government function requiring black tie and formal wear.''

"This isn't formal?" she asked, hating that her voice sounded more like a squeak.

"Good heavens, no," the princess answered.

Penny had a sinking feeling in the pit of her stomach. They were probably laughing at her—or would be soon. Her less than stylish attire made her stand out like the ugly duckling at a gathering of swans.

"So for the royal family this *is* casual?"

"I suppose you could say that," the king answered.

"I'm sorry. I didn't mean to be impertinent,'' Penny apologized, although he didn't look mad. "It's just that I have no frame of reference for this. What I meant to say is, it was most gracious of Your Highness to extend the invitation,'' she finished. "And I can see where your sons get their good looks,'' she added. One could never go wrong with a compliment.

He laughed, then gave her a courtly bow. "Farrah

is right. You are indeed a breath of fresh air. And a shameless flatterer.''

"On the contrary, Your Highness. Flattery implies a lack of sincerity, and I assure you I speak the absolute truth," she said, unable to stop her gaze from straying to Rafiq.

He looked a lot like his father, she noted. King Gamil was in his mid-fifties, but hardly looked a day over forty. It wouldn't be hollow flattery to say he could be mistaken for an older brother to his sons—the dark, dangerous and devastating threesome. The king reminded her of a distinguished movie actor. And she couldn't help wondering why he wasn't married. Or Princess Farrah, either, for that matter.

"We would like to welcome you properly to our country," he said.

The princess sipped from her crystal flute then added, "I expected Rafiq to extend the dinner invitation upon your arrival. When it became clear it had slipped his mind, I took steps to rectify the situation."

Penny figured it had slipped his mind accidentally on purpose because he was afraid she'd dump something on his expensive Armani suit. Although their working relationship was progressing smoothly, she didn't think she would live, in El Zafir or anywhere else on earth for that matter, long enough to live down the infamous coffee-spilling incident. A thousand years from now they would still talk about the klutzy American—she came, she saw, she spilled.

Just then Rafiq joined them. "Good evening, Penny," he said, bowing slightly as his father had.

"Hi." Her voice was slightly breathless, and she wished with all her heart she could blame it on descending the single flight of stairs.

"May I get you a glass of champagne?" he asked.

"Yes. Thank you. I've never tasted champagne before." It was starting. She could feel it building—the urge to talk a mile a minute. Taking a deep breath, she looked up at him and said, "Fair warning—you might want to keep your distance."

"And why would I want to do that?" he asked, the intensity of his gaze focused directly on her. "The day of your arrival was obviously not the first time you drank coffee, a fact that in no way spared my office carpet."

"I suppose it was too much to hope you might have forgotten that."

"As you have so perceptively pointed out—I listen and remember." The corners of his mouth turned up. "So I'll take my chances as you taste your first champagne."

"My son has the heart of a lion," the king said, his black eyes twinkling.

Rafiq grinned at his father, then motioned to one of the uniformed servers bearing a tray she'd wager was silver. Not silver plate, but the real McCoy that would tarnish without a gloved staff of thousands to keep it fingerprint free. She nudged her glasses more securely on her nose and took the offered crystal flute holding bubbling golden liquid.

She couldn't help feeling like the governess in a Gothic romance novel. The kind of woman who should be stashed away upstairs on important social occasions.

"Rafiq, you have been remiss in not inviting Penny to dinner sooner," the princess was saying. "It is— what is that American expression?—standard procedure for each new member of the business staff to join us, so that we can personally get to know everyone.''

''One big happy family,'' Penny commented.

''Exactly,'' the king said, smiling. ''It has become obvious over the years that contented staff are more productive. Do you think me a tyrant, Miss Doyle?''

''On the contrary, Your Highness, it's just plain, old-fashioned common sense.''

The princess touched her forearm. ''Excuse us, my dear. Gamil and I must help Johara with Fariq's twins.''

''They look fine to me,'' the older man said.

Farrah glared at him. ''Hana and Nuri are sweet children, but you know as well as I that they can easily become restless.''

The king saw her look and his eyes widened in comprehension as he nodded slightly. He bowed politely. ''My sister is correct. Excuse us, please.''

Penny glanced at Rafiq and her nerves developed nerves. So much anxiety, so little time. At work she felt in her element and had grown accustomed to dealing with him as her boss. He gave her a task, she carried it out as efficiently as possible. He didn't seem disappointed with her performance. In fact, she'd wager he wasn't the type to keep it to himself if he was displeased.

The days had fallen into a pattern. In the morning she downloaded his e-mail and printed it out, placing it on his desk. Then, allowing for time zone differences, she returned phone calls with messages from the prince, typed letters and confirmed appointments. So far, afternoons were reserved for meetings. He was in and out of the office while she fielded more phone calls and took more messages.

As she'd discussed with Rafiq, in college she'd worked at Prescott International as personal assistant to Sam Prescott, the CEO who had taught her a lot. El Zafir was a small country, but she found the tasks similar and felt completely in her element. Work was a role she could easily step into. But now the line blurred. The thought made her stomach knot.

Again she glanced up at Rafiq, hoping he would say something. She was doing her level best not to talk too much. But she completely understood the concept that silence could be deafening and was desperate to fill this one.

Finally, she couldn't stand it another moment. "At the risk of understatement, may I say, nice place you've got here. This room is exquisite."

"Thank you," he answered.

"The chandeliers are absolutely breathtaking. Although I have to tell you, I can't help wondering who keeps them so shiny. Polishing them has got to be the world's most boring job."

He looked up. "I never thought about it."

"You take it for granted. But look," she said, pointing with her champagne flute. "There must be at least a thousand crystals and each shines like a diamond teardrop. The effect is dazzling."

"Yes," he said, staring at her.

What did that mean? In the office he was all business and might as well be the fax or copy machine for all the emotion he demonstrated. But the expression in his eyes now was intense, dark, as if he could see every secret she had. Her insides quaked, or maybe it was just an aftershock from when she'd first spotted him after entering the room. Either way, she was having a difficult time curbing her natural inclination to fill the silence with anything that came to mind, as many words as she could possibly utter.

Penny looked at the place setting on the table beside her. "Are those plates edged in real gold?"

"I believe so."

Her eyes grew round. "What about the forks and knives?"

"Gold." His eyes twinkled in an expression she suspected meant he was on the verge of teasing her. "Solid. Real."

"Wow. No kidding?"

"Indeed."

"I've never seen anything as beautiful as this room. The linen on the table, the wall sconces," she said shrugging. "The flowers. Aren't those orchids along with the roses in the arrangement?"

"Yes. All real. Fresh cut. You can smell the perfume filling the air," he said, a corner of his mouth curving up. "No kidding."

"You're making fun of me."

He touched his palm to the breast of his expensive jacket, over his heart. "You wound me to the quick."

"Yeah," she said wryly. "I can almost see the blood."

"No kidding?" His smile dazzled as surely as the chandelier.

"Not me. I would never be so impertinent as to kid."

Glancing around, Penny saw his brothers, Prince Fariq and Crown Prince Kamal. His sister, Princess Johara, looked lovely in a maroon velvet long-sleeved dress that highlighted her dark hair and huge black eyes. She was nearby looking after Prince Fariq's five-year-old twins. Nuri, in a suit like his father's, and

Hana, wearing a simple green velvet dress, were completely adorable.

Even the children looked more appropriate than she. "I'm glad this is just a simple, intimate family dinner," she said.

"Why is that?"

She glanced down at her plain, inexpensive dress. "I'm not properly—"

Before she could finish the thought, there was a tinkling sound as Princess Farrah lightly tapped on crystal. "Everyone please take your places," she directed. "Dinner is about to be served. Penny, you sit right there beside Rafiq, next to Hana and Nuri."

Show time, she thought. Please don't let me spill anything, she prayed to the god of dignity and decorum.

Rafiq breathed in the scent of Penny's perfume as he held her chair. The fabric of her dress molded to her trim waist, back and hips, outlining her curves to perfection. Since the day of her arrival, he'd only seen her in shapeless dresses that did not compare favorably to her jeans. But this ordinary, inexpensive fabric was a vast improvement. He watched appreciatively as she gracefully sat.

To his disappointment, her golden hair was restrained in a twist on top of her head, but rebellious wisps caressed her slender neck. He had the most absurd desire to place his lips to an especially delicate spot just beneath her ear. Foolish thought, he chided himself. Completely inappropriate.

"Thank you." She glanced at him as he sat beside her, then pushed her glasses up more securely on her nose. "That was—the only word I can think of is *courtly*. No one's ever held a chair for me."

"You are welcome."

Considering what she'd told him about her background, that wasn't a surprise. Oddly, the information elevated her in his estimation. In her circumstances, any woman, or man for that matter, who managed to attain what she had, was strong indeed.

She sipped her champagne then placed the flute on the table. "Actually, that's not entirely true. In the orphanage a boy held my chair once. But he pulled it out when I wasn't looking and watched me fall on my fanny."

"Wretched little—"

"*Twerp* is the word you're looking for."

"I was thinking *beast*. But *twerp* will do."

He observed her but could detect no trace of self-pity. She was merely relating an experience, a practice meant to draw them closer. A bonding story. Was he required to provide chocolate? The thought made him smile. He found himself intrigued by this small woman bent but not broken by fate.

"What do you think of champagne?" he asked, observing as she sipped again.

"I'm certainly no expert, but I like it very much."

He liked teasing her. Although not in the office. Which meant he hadn't had an opportunity since her arrival. He'd found tonight's experience as pleasant as the first time. Her eyes grew round, her cheeks flushed, and the best part was anticipating her stimulating response. And he hadn't forgotten the tradition of inviting office staff to dinner. He just wasn't certain seeing Penny outside of work was wise.

The king cleared his throat and lifted his glass. "I would like you to join me in welcoming the newest staff member to our country. I believe you've all met her. Penny, may your stay with us in El Zafir be serene and peaceful.''

"Thank you, Your Highness," she said, taking a sip of her champagne.

For the next few minutes servers hovered about, placing bowls of steaming soup in front of everyone. From the corner of his eye, Rafiq watched her look around. He could almost feel waves of tension radiate from her. When everyone else began to eat, Penny tentatively touched each golden utensil, then picked up the spoon farthest from the bowl.

"So, Penny, tell me. Are you content so far?" the king asked.

Why wouldn't she be? Rafiq thought. She made a good salary. She had a roof over her head and food to eat. She was efficient and well-organized. She fit seamlessly into his office. What was there not to be content about?

Yet after he left the business wing every day, thoughts of Penny Doyle plagued him.

She looked at his father. "I am quite content, Your Highness."

"What do you think of our country?" Fariq asked.

"I haven't had an opportunity to see much. But I can say with complete honesty that this," she said, raising her hand to indicate the room, "is beautiful, nothing like where I came from."

"Tell us about the United States," Johara asked eagerly.

Penny looked at the teenager's fervent expression. "The Prescott ranch is the closest I've been to El Zafirian affluence in America. I understand you know the Prescotts."

"Very well," the king answered.

"What else did you see?" Rafiq asked.

She looked around the table, then glanced shyly at him. "Surely you don't want to hear about my boring life."

"On the contrary," his aunt Farrah said, delicately dabbing at her mouth with a linen napkin. "We would enjoy hearing everything about you."

Rafiq gave Penny his attention along with the rest of his family as she spoke of her background, obtaining her college education through scholarships, grants, student loans. The king asked how she liked Sam Prescott and if she'd met his father, Gamil's good friend. She said she had and the distraction gave her an opportunity to omit the part of her story where the jackal ran off with her inheritance. Just as well; that was no one else's business but her own. As they listened intently, the servers removed the first course and replaced it with the entrée.

"I would love to go to college in America," Johara said.

"It's too far away," her father replied sternly.

"But Kamal, Fariq and Rafiq all did," the teenager argued.

"That's different," the king responded.

"I don't see how."

Rafiq watched Penny observe his little sister's rebelliousness. It was a sore subject and one the stubborn teenager wouldn't abandon no matter how many times their father refused her request. In spite of her mutinous behavior, Johara automatically reached over and cut up Nuri's meat. The next thing he knew, Penny was doing the same to Hana's main dish.

"Thank you, Penny," the little girl said shyly.

"You're welcome," she whispered.

Kamal looked at her. "Very soon, Penny, we will make sure you see the finest sights our country has to offer. I'm sure Rafiq would be happy to give you a tour. In the meantime, tell me, what do you think of your job?"

She pushed up her glasses, but behind the thick lenses her eyes sparkled with enthusiasm. "I love it. It's challenging and keeps me very busy. I like that."

Fariq studied her. "And you have no problem working for Rafiq?"

The pulse in her throat fluttered faster as she glanced at him. "None," she said, then cleared her throat. "Already I've learned a lot from him. He is patient with my questions and an excellent teacher."

"What is he teaching you?" Kamal asked, smiling wickedly.

"Since he's the Minister of Domestic and Foreign Affairs," Penny answered, "I'm learning a lot about the affairs of El Zafir."

Both of his brothers laughed at her inadvertent double entendre. Rafiq knew they were trying to bait him. Admittedly, he'd been skeptical when his aunt had given him Penny as an assistant. But so far she'd proved herself extremely useful. He was most grateful she had shown no inclination to wait naked in his bed as the children's last nanny had done. Penny's plain, sensible approach to her work was pleasant indeed. But he was mildly surprised when he wondered if she was at all attracted to him.

"Do you miss America?" Johara asked.

Penny looked thoughtful before answering. "I don't have much to miss. So I would have to say no."

"How are plans progressing for the charity ball?" the king inquired of his sister.

"We are compiling the guest list," his sister informed him. "Only the wealthiest of the wealthy will be invited. Our goal is for the event to raise more money than ever before to feed the world's hungry children."

"It's a very worthy cause," Penny agreed. "I took a class dealing with factors that impede learning. One irrefutable truth emerged—hungry students cannot pay attention. The brain needs nutrition to function properly and assimilate information."

"Merely common sense," his aunt agreed. "I cannot think when I'm famished."

Rafiq leaned forward. This was a topic about which he felt passionately. "But it goes deeper than mere meat and potatoes. Children must feel safe and secure at every level of their existence. They can't do that if they don't know where their next meal is coming from. It's my belief that relations the world over will improve significantly when we raise a generation of children who have been properly fed and cared for. As Penny says, we must nourish their brains."

Childish laughter erupted beside him. From across the table, Fariq frowned at his children. "I see two little ones who should be concentrating harder on feeding their brains."

From the corner of his eye, Rafiq noticed movement below the tabletop. Penny had wrapped her napkin around her palm in such a way that the corners stood up like a rabbit's ears. She moved her hand to make it appear to hop. Obviously, the children were delighted.

He studied Penny. A sweet smile turned up the corners of her full mouth. Her cheeks flushed the color of pink roses, which was most becoming.

"Papa, Penny made a bunny," Hana informed her father, then dissolved into girlish giggles.

"I'm sorry," she said, holding up her impromptu puppet. "But they were wiggling, and I thought it might distract them."

"And so it did," the king commented. "Quite inventive."

"Yes," Aunt Farrah agreed. "By now they are usually too restless, and Fariq sends them back upstairs to the nanny. Where did you learn that, my dear? In one of your classes?"

Penny shook her head. "One of the social workers taught me. I was too old to be adopted, but old enough to help out with the new arrivals to the orphanage. It was a way to make the newbies smile."

Rafiq smiled, but it had nothing to do with the puppet and everything to do with the puppeteer.

When everyone finished dinner, the plates were whisked away, followed by the serving of coffee and dessert. The twins enthusiastically scooped up ice cream garnished with colorful sprinkles.

"It doesn't take much to make these two smile," commented their doting grandfather.

Had anyone ever made Penny smile? Rafiq wondered. He couldn't help feeling that she seemed far more comfortable with children than adults. And who could blame her after the way she'd been treated by the twerp who had stolen her heart and her money. An odd, unfamiliar protective feeling rose inside him, a need to shield her from any future hurt.

When the children had finished scraping the last of their dessert, Fariq looked at his watch. "It's time to go upstairs, little ones."

"Papa, no," Nuri said.

"We want to stay with Penny," Hana added.

Their father stood. "I will take you back to Crystal."

"How is the new nanny working out?" Kamal asked.

Fariq frowned. "She meets the requirements—"

"The plain stipulation," Kamal said, raising an eyebrow.

"That is the one," his brother agreed quickly. "And so far she shows no inclination that she is attracted to Rafiq. So far, so good."

But Rafiq didn't miss the strange expression on his brother's face, or the fact that he insisted on taking the children back himself instead of enlisting Johara to escort them. That was unusual indeed.

When his brother and the children were gone, Penny stood. "It's getting late. I think I'll say good-night, too."

Rafiq rose. "I hope you have enjoyed the evening."

"Very much," she said shyly.

"Penny, has Rafiq mentioned to you that the American diplomatic attaché will be visiting El Zafir several weeks from now?" Princess Farrah asked.

"Yes. I saw it on his calendar. Rafiq is scheduled to take him on a tour of the city and show him the latest in oil drilling technology."

Farrah nodded. "I'm planning a formal reception for the occasion."

All the roses washed out of Penny's cheeks. "Am I expected to attend?" Her voice was businesslike.

"You are most welcome to be present for the event."

"Is it a job requirement?" she asked.

Rafiq looked down at her. "It is not mandatory if that's what you're asking."

"Yes. I very much appreciate your gracious gesture to include me in the event," she said to the princess. "But I must most respectfully decline the invitation." She nodded a general farewell to everyone. "Now, if you'll excuse me, I'll say good-night."

Rafiq started to follow her out the door when he felt a hand on his arm. He looked down into his aunt's face. "Why do you stop me?"

"Let her go, Rafiq."

"But I wish to know why she refused to attend the reception. I desire her presence." That came out all wrong, and he hoped he was the only one to notice.

"Why is that?" his aunt wanted to know, her black eyes gleaming with keen interest.

"It will look odd if an American working in our country refuses to attend a social function for her fellow countryman." Nicely done, he thought.

"I can tell you why she turned down the invitation."

Rafiq rubbed the back of his neck. "Then I respectfully request you do so or I will follow and learn the reason myself."

"You would embarrass the poor child?" she inquired, lifting a perfectly arched eyebrow.

"Of course not. I simply wish to know her reason."

His aunt sighed as if he were dull as a butter knife. "Rafiq, you will not understand, but there is nothing simple about it."

"Of course I will understand."

His aunt sighed again. "The poor child hasn't the proper wardrobe for the affair."

The words would never pass his lips, but he did *not*

understand. What difference did it make what she wore? No one knew better than he the insignificance of attire. Beautiful women from all over the world who spent enormous amounts of money to clothe themselves in the height of fashion constantly threw themselves at him. He'd learned over and over that costly material and the latest style from high-priced designers couldn't for very long cover their shallow souls. But his aunt would not lie. That must be the source of Penny's pique.

"I will buy her something to wear," he said. "As a matter of fact, I have a business trip to Paris soon and I've toyed with the idea of taking my assistant. What better place to embellish her wardrobe?"

His aunt shook her head at him as if the dull butter knife needed sharpening. "Do not tell me again that I don't understand," he warned.

"I wouldn't dream of it," his aunt said. "I will tell you that Penny is as full of pride as you and your brothers. She will not accept that from you, not without tarnishing her soul."

"But she must attend the reception. And there are numerous functions at which I will require her presence. She will need—" he flung out his arm, frustrated at the challenges she kept raising, "—things."

His aunt smiled, and he knew it had something to do with his initial vehement protest over his new assistant. As Westerners would say, he did not wish to go there.

"I will tell you what *not* to do with a tender soul like Penny Doyle," she finally said.

Rafiq found his anticipation boundless as he waited to hear the secret to unlocking the mysteries of his new assistant.

Chapter Four

"Do not confuse a physical relationship with love," Farrah said.

This was the mysterious secret? He had never mistaken sex and love. He'd never been in love. He'd been infatuated and had come close to marrying several times. But it never felt right; the feeling never deepened the way he thought it should. Truthfully, he found that he was grateful. The experiences of his older brothers, his father and his aunt had convinced him love was a complication he would be happier without. He would simply do his duty and take a suitable wife. When he was ready.

"Forgive me, Aunt, but that makes no sense."

"Forgive me, Nephew. I didn't realize it was necessary to walk you through each step of the explanation." She sighed. "You have a certain reputation with women."

"Do not believe everything you hear."

She smiled. "I wouldn't dream of it. But Penny has

led a sheltered life. In truth, she's hardly more than a child.''

"Hardly," he said. If luck was with him, the woman who missed nothing would miss the fact that he'd just disagreed with her. Although his assistant concealed it well most of the time, he'd seen her in jeans. She was no child.

"She may have the curves of a full-grown woman," Farrah said, as if she could read his mind. "But she *is* a virgin."

He had the greatest respect for his aunt, but he was skeptical of this information. Didn't most young American women lose their virginity by the time they graduated from high school? By her own admission, Penny had a past relationship with a man—a scoundrel. Although she was too good for the swine and Rafiq was oddly bothered by the idea of her with him or any other man, surely she was no longer innocent.

"And you know this intimate detail—how?" he asked.

Farrah waved her hand dismissively. "It's obvious, Rafiq."

"Not to me. What about the man who seduced her money away? She was involved with him, and it is difficult to believe he did not seduce other things as well."

"He never touched her."

"Penny revealed this to you?" If so, chocolate worked better than alcohol to loosen a woman's tongue. However, he'd experienced the looseness of Penny Doyle's tongue and neither chocolate nor alcohol had been involved.

His aunt gave him an imperious look. "It would be indiscreet of me to say more. Suffice it to say, she has never been with a man. She arrived in El Zafir pure and innocent. It is the way she will remain.''

He met his aunt's implacable gaze with a steely-eyed look of his own that had intimidated more than one head of state. ''I am an honorable man. I do not make a practice of defiling virgins.''

She nodded. ''I have every faith in your ethics, Rafiq. You are honorable, but you are also a man. I felt it couldn't hurt to remind you to be on your best behavior.''

''I strive to always behave in a manner that will bring honor to the House of Hassan. I thank you for your interest, but the reminder is unnecessary. Good night, Aunt—''

''Wait. There's one more thing.''

''Yes?'' He gave her his attention and respect, but used every ounce of his willpower in doing so. He hadn't felt so much like a randy teenager when he'd actually been one.

''On the day Penny arrived, I gave you instructions in the manner of her treatment so that palace affairs would progress in a peaceful and serene fashion. Do you recall what I said?''

He thought for a moment. ''Do nothing out of the ordinary,'' he quoted. ''Simple courtesy in the work environment.''

''Good. Then you understand why you cannot take Penny to Paris with you.''

For reasons he didn't want to examine too closely, that directive stretched the limits of his deference. ''I do not understand at all. When I travel on business, my assistant always accompanies me. Penny works for me, and the environment goes where I go. It is nothing out of the ordinary. And though I should not need to defend myself, I feel I must remind you that I am always courteous. Therefore, it does not stretch credibility to say I can be courteous, even in Paris.''

"So you intend to fulfill the letter if not the spirit of my instructions," she said. "I would agree with you, if your assistant were a man."

"It's not my fault circumstances forced on me a female subordinate. But my needs haven't altered." She rolled her eyes and shot him a pointed look. "Ah," he said nodding, even as anger knotted inside him. "So we're back to my reputation."

"It cannot be ignored," his aunt warned. "Perhaps it's inflated. But, as the saying goes, where there's smoke, there's fire. You do indeed reap what you sow."

"I haven't sown as much as the loose-tongued gossips would have you believe." His aunt started to say something and he held up his hand. He refused to justify himself further. "I give you my word that I will not compromise Penny, in El Zafir or anywhere else."

Before he could no longer conceal his anger, he gave her a deferential bow and left the dining room. Unfortunately, he did not so easily leave behind his irritation, frustration and thoughts of his intriguing assistant.

After lunch, Penny walked from her suite through the palace on her way back to the business wing. More often than not, Rafiq had food brought into the office and they worked during the midday meal. Sometimes, like today, she ate by herself in her room. She sighed with contentment thinking about the lovely fruit salad lightly dressed with raspberry sauce. She much preferred the working lunches, but it had nothing to do with the food and everything to do with the stimulating company.

Since having dinner with the royal family a week ago, Penny had noticed a subtle difference in her boss. If she didn't know better, she would swear he was flirting with her. But she did know better. As evidenced by the loss of her money—the result of her first and, she resolved, last flirtation. That fiasco could have ended her dream of fulfilling her promise to her dying mother. Thanks to Sam Prescott for mentioning the job in El Zafir, she'd found another way to raise the necessary capital. But her close call had convinced her she couldn't let another man come between her and the vow that meant everything to her.

If only Rafiq didn't so strenuously test her resolve. The brush of his hand on her arm could be casual— or a caress. And he gave her looks that made her feel like bone-dry brush ready to go up in flames from the smallest spark.

But he was leaving for Paris later that afternoon, giving her a few days to catch her breath. And miss him a lot, she suddenly realized.

As she rounded the corner and entered the business wing, childish laughter drifted to her. She moved down the carpeted hall and entered Rafiq's office. In front of the infamous leather couch where she'd fallen asleep, she found her boss, in his expensive suit mind you, on all fours. His nephew was on his back while his niece clapped her hands and laughed at her uncle's antics.

Penny smiled. "I see you have an important business meeting."

"We're playing cowboys and Indians," the little boy informed her. "I'm a cowboy."

"I am playing the part of the cowboy's horse."

"Front or back end?" she couldn't resist asking.

"Both." Rafiq lifted one dark eyebrow as he looked at her. His expression was probably as close as a sheik could come to sheepish. "Not quite the masculine standard in your country, but—"

She laughed. "There are times, not often, but some when I wish you didn't listen and remember. Let me set the record straight—you could show a cowboy a thing or two about masculine standards. Can we be finished with all my thoughtless remarks now?"

"It would be less than gentlemanly to say no. But if you call me 'Buttercup,' I cannot be held responsible for the consequences."

"So you've seen the old Roy Rogers westerns."

"I have," he agreed.

"I'll try to refrain."

But there was something about a man playing with children—not just a man—a prince among men. She went gooey inside.

"Uncle, it's my turn," Hana said.

Nuri enthusiastically pounded his small fist on Rafiq's strong back. "Not yet. Uncle, you have to try and buck me off first."

When Rafiq reared up, the child clung to his jacket and squealed with delight. How cute was this? The ruler of a country playing with children. But she remembered how she'd hung on his every word while he passionately championed the cause of feeding hungry little ones. He'd said the world would be a better place if children everywhere were better cared for.

If he were an ordinary guy and she weren't determined to avoid any and all relationships, she would be in so much trouble. But he was who he was, and she was determined to earn back her seed money and go home. Her attraction could grow, peak and burn out. No trouble; no danger. Neat, simple, quiet—and ultimately not up for debate.

"Well, what have we here?"

She turned and smiled at Crystal Rawlins, the children's dark-haired nanny. It was difficult to ascertain the color of her eyes behind the glasses. As Penny pushed her own spectacles more securely onto her nose, she couldn't help thinking there seemed to be an epidemic of weak-eyed American women enlisted to work in El Zafir.

"Hi, Crystal. Rafiq is doing his impression of a bucking bronco for the children. But under no circumstances are we allowed to call him 'Buttercup.'"

The other woman grinned and nodded. "Roy Rogers, huh?"

"Indeed," Rafiq said. How *did* he manage to maintain his dignity under the circumstances? "I see you two have met," he said, glancing between herself and the nanny.

"Yes," Penny answered for both of them. "My room in the guest quarters is very close to Crystal's in the family wing. We see each other frequently."

He looked at the nanny. "Are you recovered from your adventure in the desert?"

Penny had heard about Fariq and Crystal getting trapped in the desert. Thanks to modern technology and communications, they were never in any danger, but it had been safer to stay put than try to return to the palace. Penny imagined the experience was very exciting, and wished, albeit briefly, that she could be alone anywhere with Rafiq.

"There was nothing to recover from," Crystal said

to the prince. "Fariq and I were riding in the desert and a huge sandstorm caught us by surprise. We were stuck in the tent overnight. No big deal."

"I heard." He rose gracefully to his feet in spite of the fact that Nuri still clung tightly to his neck. "My brother was wise to take refuge until the storm ended. It is easy to lose the way under those conditions. Landmarks are obscured, including the stars. The desert has claimed many who were foolish enough to ignore its dangers."

Penny leaned against her desk. "Even here in the palace with sturdy walls around us, the storm was a bit frightening. A flimsy tent must have been really bad."

Crystal smiled. "I wouldn't describe the royal tent as flimsy—just picture roughing it El Zafirian style. But it was a little scary. I'm glad the children were safe here in the palace."

"Their Aunt Johara willingly pitched in. As did everyone." Rafiq turned his head and grinned at his nephew peeking over his shoulder. Then he gently touched his niece's cheek with one finger. "It was no hardship to spend time with these two."

Crystal nodded. "I'm so relieved. Children are often shuffled off to staff." She laughed, her humor self-deprecating. "I guess that's me—staff. But somehow I don't feel like the hired help. What I'm trying to say is that it's refreshing to see a family so interested in the children's welfare."

"It is the way of this family," Rafiq said in his why-would-you-question-it tone. "And of my brother in particular. Fariq values his children above everything."

Penny thought Crystal's cheeks flushed a becoming

pink at the mention of Prince Fariq. She wondered if the sandstorm was the only danger the nanny had encountered. For reasons she didn't understand, Penny preferred Rafiq's good looks. But Prince Fariq was also very handsome, in an intense sort of way.

Rafiq looked at Crystal and smiled. "I would be happy to entertain the children again sometime, if you would like an afternoon off to see the sights of the city."

The nanny warmly returned his smile. "That's very kind. Tales of your—that is to say, stories about you— in the tabloids, I mean. Well, what I'm trying to say is that I'm sure your reputation must have been exaggerated."

"My aunt chose wisely when she hired you."

Penny's first thought was—your aunt chose me, too. Wasn't that wise? The twinge of jealousy almost distracted her from her second thought—was she missing something in this conversation? She'd read about the playboy prince. But to her he had been nothing but unfailingly cordial and polite. Surely any hint of flirtation was nothing more than her imagination coupled with the tiniest bit of wishful thinking. He didn't seem the sort to play games. If anyone would be able to spot insincerity, it was her.

"I'll take these two little ones off your hands now," Crystal said as Rafiq easily swung the little boy off his back. "Come, Hana, Nuri. It's story time."

"Ya-ay," the twins said at the same time.

After Crystal ushered the children from the room, Rafiq was alone with Penny. He looked at his assistant and thought about the Fates that had allowed his brother a night in the desert with a young woman, albeit a plain one, as stipulated in the nanny requirements.

Penny had applied for the same job under the same requirements. However, the longer he knew her, the less plain he thought her. And the prospect of getting his assistant all to himself was most pleasant. Perversely, it had grown more so since his aunt's warning. Or was he merely excessively intrigued because Farrah had pointed out Penny's innocence? He knew she was less worldly than the women he was accustomed to. Yet he had difficulty believing she was completely pure and innocent. Irritation grew within him. Without question, he spent far too much time thinking about his small assistant with the large glasses.

Penny's generous mouth turned up at the corners even as a puzzled expression crossed her face. "I can't help wondering...." She straightened away from the desk and turned her back to him as she busied herself with papers.

"What?"

"It's none of my business," she said.

Since when did his assistant censor herself? Now he was most curious. "I insist you speak your mind."

"Okay. You asked for it."

Penny twisted around and met his gaze, and he somehow knew she wouldn't ask her original question. But the shadows in her blue eyes were magnified and he wondered what was making her sad.

"What is it, Penny?"

"It's going to be awfully quiet around here after you leave for Paris."

"You will miss me?"

"Yes," she said simply.

His spirit soared. Because his temptation for her

grew daily, he'd wrestled with the problem of whether or not it was wise for Penny to accompany him on the trip. Now he'd learned his brother had been alone in the desert with the nanny. Granted, fate had intervened. But Rafiq would be conducting business and his trusted assistant would be invaluable. Penny would have her own room in the hotel.

He thought about a chaperon but immediately rejected the idea as unnecessary. He never confused love and sex. The first had never happened to him and he didn't expect it would now; the second was out of the question because he'd given his word. So what harm could there be in taking her with him? Then there was her comment that he would be missed. How could he leave her behind?

"Would you like to go to Paris with me? No kidding," he said when she looked doubtful, as if he were teasing her.

"Paris? France?"

"I believe that's where it is located."

"But your plane is scheduled to leave—" She glanced at the watch on her slender wrist again. "You're supposed to be at the airport in two hours."

"Yes?"

"I'd have to pack."

"Yes?"

"It's too quick. What if I forget something?"

"I've heard there is shopping in Paris," he said wryly. "You will have everything you need. So it's all arranged."

She put a hand to her forehead, as if her thoughts were spinning. "This is so sudden. I mean, I wish you'd said something sooner."

"I was—" What? Forbidden by his aunt? He was

Prince Rafiq Hassan, Minister of Domestic and Foreign Affairs. If he wanted his assistant to accompany him on a business trip, that's what would happen. He need not explain himself. "You will accompany me."

She clapped her hands together, not unlike one of the twins. "I'm going to Paris!"

The excitement on her face had made her almost beautiful. Yet he knew that was not what produced the odd feeling in his chest, followed by the need to take a deep breath of air into his lungs. He'd had the most absurd desire to pull her into his arms. Before he could, she'd raced out of the office.

Apparently, the prospect of spending time alone with him didn't bother her. Obviously, she trusted him. That was good. Perhaps she thought of him as she might an older brother. That was bad. And the fact it was probably for the best did nothing to sweeten his suddenly sour mood.

If there was an inoculation against sensory overload, Penny didn't want it. From the moment she'd stepped aboard the royal family's private jet, complete with reclining leather seats and bedroom, she'd received a crash course in lifestyles of the rich and famous. On the way to the hotel they'd passed the Eiffel Tower and the Arc de Triomphe. Before that, Rafiq had insisted their driver take them to Versailles. He'd grinned when she'd said his family home in El Zafir was quite large and lovely but no one could do decadence like the French.

Then there was the hotel—simply put, it was elegant and beautiful. Marble floors, Persian rugs, satin-covered furniture, gold fixtures, crown moldings and flowers everywhere. She even had her own spacious suite, complete with large, lovely bath and king-size bed in the separate bedroom beyond the sitting area. And there was a connecting door to Rafiq's room. Between the two of them, they occupied one whole floor of the hotel.

This was her second day in the city. The previous twenty-four hours had been a blur of business meetings followed by a working dinner. That morning they'd toured an orphanage and homeless shelters in a part of Paris the travel industry wouldn't advertise to tourists. The evidence of poverty broke her heart. Rafiq had issued a personal invitation for a French representative to attend El Zafir's Feed the Children charity event.

Penny had been resting in her room with her feet up when a knock sounded on her door. A French woman had breezed in trailed by an assistant hauling a rack of clothes. The aggressive woman had told her His Royal Highness, Prince Rafiq Hassan, had ordered her, Madame Gisele, to bring a variety of clothing that she thought his assistant would enjoy trying on. Without obligation, she'd said.

Penny couldn't have been more delighted. She'd toured the city. Now she had an opportunity to sample some of the fashions. And how thoughtful of Rafiq. She could simply try them on without the awkward, embarrassing part of finding a diplomatic way to let the woman know she couldn't afford to buy a pair of socks, let alone an outfit from such an expensive boutique. In the bedroom, she now stood with mirrors on three sides as Madame Gisele fussed over her. Penny looked at herself dressed in a double-breasted black jacket trimmed in white with a matching slim skirt skimming her knee.

"This is perfect," she said, sighing. The outfit made her look *good*. Too bad she would never own something so stylish. In the mirror she studied the woman's beaming expression. Maybe she should just clarify the fact that Madame Gisele was barking up the wrong tree, the one money *didn't* grow on. "But it's far too expensive for my limited funds."

Madame waved her hand dismissively. "Do not give it another thought."

Penny sighed. Spoken by a woman who didn't have to worry about such things. At least she could relax because there was no doubt they were now on the same page.

"How did you know this would fit?" she asked.

"His Royal Highness commanded petite sizes. I must say he was—how do you say—right on." The dark-haired, brown-eyed woman who looked to be in her late forties nodded approvingly. She brushed her hands over the shoulders of the jacket and down the hips of the skirt. "He has much experience sizing up women, no?"

"No. That is to say, I guess. Actually, I have no idea."

"He is a man among men. If I were twenty years younger… To be the lucky woman to capture the heart of such a man," Madame said. Then her dreamy look faded, replaced by businesslike appraisal as she sized up Penny's reflection. "So you like this one, too?"

"I adore everything you brought, Madame."

"Excellent. Now for the cocktail dresses and evening gowns."

Penny tried on several dresses, some knee-length, others that skimmed her ankles, all elegant and modest and a perfect fit. Finally Madame riffled through the rack of plastic-protected clothes. "Here."

Penny looked at the strapless black dress in ecstasy. "Wow."

"Indeed, wow. Try it on, chérie."

Penny stepped out of a full-length, long-sleeved, high-necked shimmering silver number and Madame took it from her to hang up. Then she handed over the black temptation. Realizing she needed to lose her bra, Penny excused herself and went into the bathroom, leaving the door open a crack.

"So innocent," the woman said. "You think I have not seen everything you have a hundred times?"

"Not on me specifically," Penny said, refusing to apologize for her modesty.

The dress was light as air. Of course the fact that there was so very little material on top could have had something to do with it. She stepped into the soft, silky material and realized she couldn't fasten the back.

Clutching the abbreviated top to her breasts, she stepped into the bedroom without looking up. "Madame, would you mind hooking me? I couldn't—oh!"

Rafiq stood there. She hadn't heard him come in. Her cheeks burned. She couldn't bear to look at herself in the mirrors and know for a fact the blush on her face showed on her chest, too. But since her gaze was drawn to him and she couldn't have looked away if her life depended on it, there was no danger of seeing the evidence of her own embarrassment.

"His Royal Highness asked to be informed when you were modeling this gown," Madame explained.

Rafiq's eyes darkened dangerously. "Turn," he said, making a circular motion with one finger. "I will fasten the back."

She did as ordered. In the mirror she watched his gaze lower to the task. His warm breath stirred her hair and fanned her shoulders, making her shiver. She felt the brush of his hands and expected to hear a hiss as if the heated touch would leave a brand in their wake. Instead, there was the whisper of the zipper as he raised it, pulling the sides of the dress snugly around her. Although it seemed like slow motion, far too quickly his lean, strong fingers completed the task and she let out a long breath.

She should feel more secure, but nothing could have been further from the truth as she caught a glimpse of herself in the mirror. The full-length lace dress kissed the carpet and covered her breasts, but she still felt *exposed.* It had nothing to do with the garment and everything to do with the way he seemed to see into her soul.

He raised his hands and removed the pins holding her hair in its conservative twist. The blond strands instantly cascaded around her face and shoulders. He lifted her glasses from her nose and handed them to Madame, who deposited them on the dresser, then discreetly left the room. They were alone.

"Lovely," he breathed, filling his hands with her hair, then settling it down her back. "I knew it would be."

"You picked this?" she asked, lifting the skirt's lace overlay away from the silk lining hugging her body.

"I picked everything. Gisele faxed me sketches of the items she had in mind, and I made the final choices."

"You have excellent taste." Penny couldn't breathe and it had nothing to do with the fact that her bodice was so tight she couldn't have flashed him even if she'd wanted to.

Rafiq was too close, too warm, too handsome, too everything for her pathetically inadequate respiratory system.

"I know what I like. If that is good taste…" He shrugged.

"Is there anything you're not good at?"

"No."

Without her glasses, her image in the mirror was slightly fuzzy. Penny brushed her palms down the soft material of the skirt. "I had a fabulous time trying everything on, but why would you go to so much trouble? It's all going back to the boutique—"

At that moment, Madame Gisele fluttered back into the room. "Your Highness, everything you chose fit her like a dream. No alterations are required."

"Good," he said, nodding as he continued to stare at her reflection. "Send everything to the plane. We will take it with us when we leave this evening."

"What?" Penny said, whirling around to face him. So much for smoke and mirrors. The spell was definitely broken.

He met her gaze and one of his dark eyebrows lifted. "You required appropriate apparel for the diplomatic reception. Now you have it." He turned to walk out of the room.

"Not so fast, Your Worship," she said.

Chapter Five

"Your Worship?" Rafiq knew sarcasm. Something was wrong with her but he had no idea what it could be.

"Now that I have your undivided attention, you can't have all those clothes sent to the plane."

"I can and I have," he answered patiently. "In fact, you heard me give the order. It is already done."

"Then you can just unorder it. I can't pay for those things," she said, her big blue eyes growing bigger and bluer with what looked like alarm.

"So that is what's troubling you," he said, relieved. "I have arranged for the bill to be sent to me."

"And you think that's all there is to it?"

"Yes."

Her alarm disappeared, replaced by another emotion he would have to call irritation. Puzzling. What did she have to be irritated about? She now had a complete wardrobe.

"Yes? That's all you can say?" She planted her

hands on her black-lace-clad hips and glared at him, obviously piqued.

Even vexed, maybe because of it, she was completely and utterly delightful. He couldn't take his eyes from the sight of her. The angry rise and fall of her chest drew his attention to the exquisite way she filled out the top of the dress. He'd pictured her in this creation, but the reality was far lovelier than the fantasy. Blood raced hot and fast through his veins.

"There is nothing else *to* say." Surely the harsh, husky hoarse tone surrounding his words was caused by Paris air pollution and endless talk in meetings that had taken a toll on his voice. What else would explain it?

"That makes one of us because *I* have lots to say. Starting with—this seems completely inappropriate to me."

"On the contrary, it is completely appropriate. You needed clothing for official palace and business functions. Now you have it."

"If you're worried that I'll embarrass you, or anyone else in the royal family, don't be. I intend to be a credit to the House of Hassan and to El Zafir. I plan to shop when my bank account is sufficiently padded."

"There's no need. You've already shopped."

"No. *You* shopped. One of those outfits would set me back—well, more than I want to think about. It's not that I can't afford even a couple of those things. I just won't do it at the expense of my dream."

"The preschool," he confirmed. "Do not worry. Your dream is secure. You need sacrifice nothing."

This wasn't going at all as he'd planned. In his experience, only jewelry generated more gratitude than an article of clothing created by a noted Paris designer. He'd just purchased a complete wardrobe for Penny and angered her in the process. He was not in the habit of defending his actions, especially about something so trivial. Was it Americans in general or this woman in particular he did not understand?

"You're right about not sacrificing. Because the clothes will remain with Madame Gisele."

"I have already told you the cost will be taken care of." He put just the right amount of finality in his tone to end the conversation.

But when Penny shook her head, not unlike the way Aunt Farrah had done when announcing the secret to dealing with his assistant, he knew she wasn't finished with the matter. His revered aunt must have left out the most important secret, because dealing with Penny was going badly.

"Since when did I turn into a doll you can dress up? Barbie and I are nothing alike. I'm a completely different body type—no long legs or big..." She put her hands far out in front of her bosom to indicate where she was lacking.

Rafiq thought she looked perfect. The barest swell of her breasts was visible. They were small, round and firm, and the skin looked smooth and soft. Just right. He would give much to know the texture and taste of her. His fingers tingled and his palms itched to touch her, but he dared not. He would not give in to temptation at the risk of hurting her.

He reminded himself that clothes did not make the man—or woman. While this dress revealed Penny's physical attributes in a most positive way, it did not disclose the true character of her heart. As he studied the stubborn set of her mouth and angry tilt of her

chin, he knew *that* was an example of her nature.
Oddly enough, he liked what he saw. His blood stirred
again at the spirit swirling in her flashing blue eyes.
Although he could do without *this* manifestation of her
pride. It didn't sweeten his rapidly deteriorating dis-
position when he recalled his aunt's warning about this
very thing.

"If I'm supposed to be plain, there's no reason for
me to dress to the nines."

"A plain *nanny* was required. That's not the position for which you were hired. There is every reason
for you to dress as befits my assistant." Technically,
his aunt's assistant, a fact which he chose to overlook
just now.

"Still, clothes do not make the man—or woman."

"I agree." He'd thought the very same thing only
moments ago. Perhaps that was a good sign this discussion was coming to a successful conclusion.

"Then I don't see why it's a big deal," she said,
twisting her fingers together in agitation. "Designer
clothes will not make a difference in the way I perform
my duties as your assistant."

"I do not know what troubles you." He would try
one more time to explain, he decided, tamping down
his irritation. He infused his tone with as much patience as he could gather. "Do not misunderstand,
Penny. This isn't personal. There are numerous official
and very public functions at which I require your presence. Your appearance is a reflection on El Zafir as
long as you are in my employ. As you are a most
intelligent woman, no doubt you understand this. My
aunt informed me that your refusal to attend the diplomatic reception was because of your own apparel

limitations. And now I have removed those limitations. This is about duty, job and country.''

''Oh?'' she asked, lifting an eyebrow.

Without her glasses he could see the expression in her eyes and almost wished he couldn't. ''Yes. If you ran out of paper clips, staples or computer paper, I would supply it.''

''So designer dresses are nothing more to you than office supplies?''

''Exactly,'' he said, smiling. ''I knew you learned quickly.''

''Not as quickly as you think. The clothes I wear feel very personal to me and are something I should pay for myself. But the cost of what you chose would be a big chunk of money that I could use toward building my preschool. I won't spend it frivolously. Thank you for the offer, but I can't accept them.''

''I am your employer, and I order you to take them.''

This was beyond his experience, he thought, running a hand through his hair. Since when did a sheik, the family charmer, have to order a woman to accept clothing—or anything else for that matter? And why was it so important that she did accept? His motives were not something he wanted to think about at the moment. Dealing with this stubborn American was more important. Perhaps a little flattery. Or as Penny would say, a sincere compliment.

''You look quite lovely in this dress. Although it is a bit too revealing even for the diplomatic reception to welcome the American attaché.''

''Good. It's the most expensive of the lot. I can't afford it.''

"I can. And I will. It will be on the plane when we leave for El Zafir."

"Even if I'm not?"

Her words produced a coldness inside him that spread quickly. The idea of returning to El Zafir without her was unacceptable. "Why wouldn't you?" He met her gaze. "The royal palace pays well, and it will finance your dream."

Her mouth thinned to a straight line as her shoulders relaxed slightly in what he hoped was capitulation. "When you're right, you're right. And a promise is a promise," she murmured. "I can't afford to lose my job over this."

"Very well."

She started to walk past him. "I'll see if Madame Gisele will unzip me—"

He curved his fingers around her slender upper arm to stop her. "Do not bother. I will assist you."

His breathing grew most unsteady at the feel of her soft, warm skin. He dropped his hand and found the zipper, taking care to touch only that thin piece of metal. If his fingers encountered any more of her soft flesh...but touch wasn't the only one of his senses she challenged.

The sight of the creamy curve of her spine, revealed as the material parted, caused sweat to bead on his forehead. It was a good thing the plane was waiting. Another night with her on the other side of a connecting door might well be more than his rapidly diminishing willpower could endure.

Holding the black lace to her breasts, Penny turned toward him. "If this little number stretches the envelope on El Zafir's conservative dress code, I don't understand why you insist on bringing it with us. I won't pay for it. I'll never wear it."

She disappeared into the bathroom. The door closing was followed by a loud click, indicating she'd locked it, cutting off his reminder that the dress was already bought and paid for.

"You're wrong, little one. You will wear it again," he whispered.

But he would be the only man to see.

Penny walked into her office and sat down behind her desk. She and Rafiq had returned late the previous evening from the whirlwind trip to Paris. It felt like a fantasy, until she looked at the designer duds hanging in her closet. She didn't get it. Why would he spend so much money?

Of course. It was about appearances and the pride of El Zafir as a nation. Not about her. Or fairy tales.

But a tiny part of her so wished it was.

Which was why she was determined to keep the incident in perspective. Besides, he'd won that battle, but she had the distinct feeling this was war and there would be more skirmishes before either of them raised the white flag.

She heard voices from down the hall and recognized Rafiq's. Touching the back and sides of her hair to make sure it was tidy, she braced herself to face him as she pushed her glasses more firmly on her nose.

He rounded the corner and stepped into the room. She smiled, even as her heart thumped painfully in her chest.

"Good morning, Rafiq," she said brightly. "Shall I call for coffee to be brought?"

"Good morning," he answered, staring at her.

"You did not have sufficient time to recuperate from traveling?"

"I am quite rested and raring to go. Let me check your schedule—"

"So you are working today?"

"Of course. Why would you ask?"

"You are not dressed for it."

"On the contrary." She looked down at her khaki dress, the one she'd worn on her first day. She'd wondered if he would notice and say anything. And if so, how long it would take. She had her answer, which was not very darn long. "I am appropriately attired for today."

"Why are you not attired in something new?"

There was the sixty-four-thousand-dollar question. Could she make him understand? A girl who grew up as she had couldn't afford to look a gift horse in the mouth any more than she could afford designer clothes from Paris. To him it was insignificant because he had more money than God. To her, it struck at the very cornerstone of her foundation—you never get something for nothing.

A man had paid attention to her once before and she'd believed he loved her. She'd also believed him with all her heart when he'd told her he could double her inheritance. She could start her preschool in her mother's name to keep her memory alive, and turn a profit for their future. But he took the money and ran. It was a painful lesson, and she'd learned it well. When a man paid attention to her, even if that man was a prince, look out. Nothing and no one would get in the way of her goal again.

"If you're worried that I'll bring shame on you—"

"No."

"Good." She swiveled her chair to look at her computer monitor. "The schedule is light today. I purposely booked it that way because of your trip. There are no outside visitors or appointments on your agenda. Consequently, no one but you will see me in this—"

"Unflattering garment," he interjected.

"If the shoe fits…"

"I had hoped to see you in something else."

"And for a business day like this one I preferred to wear my own clothes instead of job-related apparel."

"So you don't plan on working?"

"Of course I do. In my own things. It's called balance—a word that I think is foreign to you."

"I have heard of this word. Yet I find your manner of demonstrating its meaning refreshing if a bit baffling."

"I live to baffle."

One corner of his wonderful mouth lifted, making her pulse flutter. He was teasing her. Wasn't that a good thing? She hadn't realized how much she'd feared angering him until he wasn't angry at all. He was a nice man. It would have been so much easier if he wasn't. Her life had been a series of hard knocks and her own stupid mistakes. Hard knocks she could take as they came. Stupid mistakes she learned not to repeat. She had no intention of getting sucked in by a sheik in sheep's clothing. But in case he was as nice as he seemed, now would be a good time to put up her defenses.

Unfortunately, he picked that moment to smile, and her heart dropped to her toes, making it tough to fortify a moving target. It was like riding a roller coaster;

it made her feel out of control. She hated the feeling and the best way to deal with it was not to get on.

"Since the schedule is light today, I think I will take this rare opportunity to go for a ride," he announced out of the blue.

Talk about living to baffle. But again she managed to put a cheerful smile on her face. "Good idea. I'll hold down the fort while you go—"

"I'd like you to come with me."

"I...don't know what to say." She pressed her palm to her chest. "A drive would be nice but—"

"Not cars. Horses."

"Horseback riding? Of course."

If she'd needed another reminder of how different they were, she'd just gotten it. Naturally, he'd meant on a horse. What was she thinking? It was a sport royalty embraced just because they could. Average, ordinary, run-of-the-mill folks like herself didn't have the money to indulge in the expensive pastime.

"You've ridden before?" he asked.

"No. Yes. I mean once or twice. When I was in the orphanage we were invited to a ranch and had the opportunity to ride lobotomized horses that wouldn't maim or kill us. But that was a long time ago."

"And this is where you met cowboys?" he asked, his intensity quotient cranking up.

She smiled. "Not exactly."

"Then where?"

"School. Grocery store. On the street. In bars."

"You went to bars?"

She laughed. "No. I just threw that out to see if you were still listening. I didn't have time to indulge—too busy working, going to school and studying."

"All the more reason for you to accompany me."

"How's that?"

"I'm offering you the opportunity to—let your hair down, as you Americans say." His gaze seemed to grow hotter as it settled on her conservative hairstyle.

But she had bigger fish to fry than handling the heat of his expression and how it made her feel. He wanted her to spend time with him outside work. Not an especially good idea after discovering she had to erect defenses against Prince Charming and his smile. If horses were involved when he smiled at her—look out. She could wind up on her backside in the dirt.

"I have work to do," she said.

One dark eyebrow lifted. "There is a word I have just recently learned. It's called *balance*—it means to bring into harmony or proportion. In other words, to invest the same amount of time and energy into play as one does in work. So far, you have not balanced your time between the two equally."

"Obviously, it's unnecessary to test your listening skills," she muttered. "So you're saying all work and no play makes Penny a dull employee?"

He grinned. "Exactly so."

"I appreciate what you're trying to do. But you said it's rare that you get the opportunity to ride. I don't know how. Surely you don't want me slowing you down."

"I will teach you."

"I don't know—"

"You do not wish to learn?"

"Oh, no. That's not it at all, quite the opposite. But it's not necessary for you to be involved—"

"So you do not wish *me* to teach you?"

"Oh, no. It was not my intention to insult you. I just don't want to take up your valuable time in such a tedious undertaking. On this rare opportunity for you to have fun and happy good times, you should enjoy yourself.''

"And you think it would not be enjoyable teaching you to ride?''

"How could it be?''

"Leave it to me to decide what is and is not enjoyable.''

"Okay.''

"So your answer is yes?'' he asked again.

"My answer is I have nothing to wear.''

"Your jeans will do.''

"I didn't think they would be appropriate.''

"They would be most appropriate.''

Busted. She had no excuse.

"So, your answer is yes?''

How could she say no? He was her boss. She was dying to go riding, and he'd left her no diplomatic way out. And why in the world was she agonizing over this? Surely his patience with a beginner would evaporate quickly and he'd either end the lesson or turn her over to someone else.

"My answer is—okay.''

But when she looked at him, the way his eyes sparked when he'd told her to wear jeans, her heart cranked into high gear. So what else was new?

Not a darn thing. Surely going riding with him would be no different from one-on-one time here in the office.

Chapter Six

Rafiq held the bridle and absently stroked the horse's neck as he looked up at Penny. "You are certain you're not afraid? I would be agreeable to riding double until you become used to your mount and feel safe."

She grinned. "That's not necessary. I feel great. The horse feels great. Maybe I was a cowgirl in a past life. Either you're a very good teacher, or I've just taken to this whole riding thing like a duck to water."

Disappointment seared through him as he studied her glowing eyes and cheeks flushed with excitement. His heart raced at the sight of her. They were in an enclosure just outside the stables on the palace grounds. The weather hovered somewhere between winter and spring, which for El Zafir meant quite pleasant. For the past hour he'd been instructing his athletically gifted assistant in the basics of riding a horse. And none of that explained to his satisfaction what it was about this woman that fascinated him so.

He'd heard it said what a man *couldn't* see intrigued him. Perhaps the glasses hiding her face tantalized him. Or the jeans he'd requested her to wear. He glanced at her leg, so close to where his hand rested on the horse's neck. Maybe the denim encasing the shapely curves and soft flesh was in fact invested with magical properties to befuddle a man unaccustomed to being befuddled by any woman.

What he needed was a stimulating ride to clear his head. "If you're sure…"

"Very. I'm not ready to race across the desert. Maybe tomorrow," she said, smiling.

He grinned in response. "Very well. As much as I would like to ride like the wind, I will curb my usual breakneck pace to accommodate you. As they say in your country, let's take these babies out and see what they can do." He swung into his own saddle.

As much as he wanted to give his horse its head and ride as if the devil were after him, he didn't dare. Penny's mount would follow his own and her inexperience would be a problem. And he couldn't leave her alone—even if he wanted to, which he did not—because the desert could be unforgiving for an innocent like his assistant. So much for a stimulating ride. What was he thinking? Apparently, he wasn't, a state for which Penny Doyle, rhymes with oil, was entirely responsible.

And why had she refused to wear the clothes he'd purchased?

Sometimes it was more soothing to go from the vaguely disquieting to the incomprehensible. He'd never encountered such a puzzle with any other woman. Every one he'd ever known had gratefully accepted anything he chose to give.

Penny looked around and sighed. "It's such a glorious day."

"It is indeed."

As the horses walked, she breathed deeply of the cool, fresh air. How he wished the movement didn't draw his notice to her bosom and torment him so. Her cotton shirt molded in a most agreeable way to her chest. How like Penny to have perky breasts. As much as he tried to maintain neutrality, his hands ached to know the exact shape and texture of her body.

Glancing up, she said, "I don't believe I've ever seen a bluer sky anywhere. Not even in Texas."

"And Texas sets the standard in skies as it does in cowboys?" he asked, looking over at her as they swayed side by side in their saddles.

"You're never going to let me forget that, are you?"

"No."

Nor could he forget his aunt telling him her college diploma meant she was very trainable and capable of learning. Today he wished she wasn't quite so teachable; her trepidation would have given him an excuse to put his arms around her. Something he would very much like to do. Because it would give him close proximity to the graceful column of her neck, which he was certain possessed as many mysteries as an uncharted oasis. He cursed the fact that he'd seen her slender, creamy shoulders bared in the black dress he'd chosen in Paris. The memory stirred his already agitated senses.

"Tease me if you must, but the sky is the bluest I've ever seen."

"I'm glad you are pleased. I ordered this day especially for you."

She laughed. "You're good, but I don't think even *you* are that good."

Her radiant smile was like an arrow piercing to the very heart of him. He *was* good and how he wished he could show her—train her. He didn't believe she was quite the innocent his aunt had said, but neither was she very cosmopolitan. What he wouldn't give to instruct her in the ways of the world, the sensuous dance between a man and a woman.

What was he thinking? His reputation in the palace remained in tatters because of a woman unable to control herself. The household was just recovering from an uproar for which he'd been blamed but, in truth, hadn't been his fault. Now he was contemplating something far worse. *Contemplate* was too benign a word. His body was on fire for her, sparking the temptation to compromise an employee. And not just any employee, one he'd been expressly forbidden to touch.

"My goodness," Penny said.

He met her puzzled gaze. "Yes?"

"You're looking terribly fierce about something."

"I was thinking about riding.…"

"What about it?" she asked, frowning.

"That I would like to go…faster."

She frowned. "If you want to ride like the wind, go for it. You already explained the horse is trained to find the way back to the stables. Don't give me another thought."

He would like that. Unfortunately, it was proving a difficult task.

"No," he said. "But I would like to pick up the pace. There's something I would like to show you. Do you think you're ready to go a bit faster?"

She grinned. "There's nothing I would like better."

Oh, little one, he thought. Never challenge a man such as myself who is aching to go faster with you.

"Your wish is my command," he said, applying gentle pressure to his horse.

The mount sprang forward, trained by his own hand to react to even the most subtle command. Penny's horse did the same. There was a look of concentration on her face, an expression she used when she struggled to remember every word of his direction to execute a task perfectly. Would she look the same if he kissed a soft, delicate spot just beneath her ear and told her what would please him in return?

As the sensuous vision formed, he thoughtlessly jerked his horse's reins, then had to settle the restless animal. If he neglected his own concentration, he could break his fool neck. Which was why he'd decided to ride in the first place, in order to occupy his mind with something other than Penny. Now would be a good time to do that.

They rode in silence until the shimmering waves rising off the golden sand gave way to green grass, palm trees and water that glistened like diamonds in the sun.

"An oasis," Penny said, delighted.

"Yes."

"Are we stopping here?"

"Yes," he said again, slowing his horse.

Rafiq brought the animal to a halt beneath the spreading branches of a palm beside the small lake. He slipped out of the saddle and tied the animal to the tree. Taking Penny's reins he did the same for her. Instantly both horses dropped their heads and began to graze.

Penny started to dismount and swung her leg over

the back of the saddle. Coming up behind her, he put his hands at her waist and easily lowered her to the ground, letting her backside slide down his front. Her slight tremble told him she noticed the intimate contact.

"Come, let us cool off by the water."

"That sounds lovely."

Before leading her to the crystal-clear lake, he took two bottles of water from his saddlebag. Kneeling on the grass, he dipped his hands into the water, then brushed the cool liquid over his face and the back of his neck. Penny did the same, then took the bottle he handed her and drank deeply. Moisture clung to her lips and he wanted to lick it away. How he wished he were a less honorable man. Or that he hadn't drawn the line in the sand and reminded his aunt so forcefully that Penny would be safe with him. And she would be safe—from other men or any harm. But what harm could he, Rafiq, do to her?

She brushed the back of her hand over her moist lips. "This place is unbelievable. Such beauty. In the middle of the desert."

"Such beauty indeed," he said, meeting her gaze without looking away.

Her blue eyes narrowed as she looked at him. "Are you making fun of me?"

He blinked and stared at her, his own eyes narrowing. "Why would you think such a thing?"

"The way you're looking at me. And what you just said. You implied—but that can't be true so you must be laughing at me."

"I would never do such a thing. And I do think you're quite lovely." He rested his forearm on his knee as he stared at her. "You are also spirited and smart. I'm in a constant state of anticipation—'' that would not reassure her ''—to hear what you'll say next,'' he added quickly.

''I'm glad. A girl like me has to work harder.''

''Harder? Why? What do you mean 'a girl like you'?''

''Plain. Not that I'm complaining. In life you play the hand you're dealt. Maximize your strengths.'' She plucked a blade of grass and pulled at it. ''Someone pretty can walk into a room and be enough, by virtue of her looks. Instead of relying on my face to get noticed, I use my head, remember things people say, try to be witty, you know.'' She laughed. ''On second thought, how could you? You're a beautiful man.''

He laughed. ''That is not an adjective a man normally aspires to.''

''You know what I mean. Not only are you more handsome than the average bear, er, sheik, but you're a natural people person to boot. There's no way you could bond with me in overcoming the insecurity of what it feels like to be homely, shy and insignificant.''

''I could provide chocolate,'' he offered, anything to take the clouds out of her blue eyes. Why did the big ugly glasses not hide that?

''And you're considerate, too. Like I said before, is there anything you're not good at?''

Yes, he wanted to say. He was very bad at resisting the forbidden. Because more than anything he wanted to chase the shadows from her face, and there was only one way he could think to do it.

''Penny—'' He stood up, then reached a hand down to her. She took it and he pulled her to her feet and into his arms.

"What are you doing?" she whispered. Her mouth trembled but she didn't pull away.

"I am going to kiss you." He removed her glasses and tucked them in his back pocket. Then he lifted her arm to his shoulder. "I will not hurt you."

"I know."

He wanted to ask how she knew. He wanted to warn her not to be so trusting. *He* would take great care, but there were other men who...but she knew that. And he could wait no longer to taste her lips.

Lowering his mouth to hers, he tunneled his fingers into her hair, savoring the feel of the silken strands. The first touch of her trembling lips was cloud soft and honey sweet, sweeping him away on a magic carnal carpet. Instantly his heart thundered in his chest, threatening to fly free of the confines.

He lifted his head and studied her face, her beautiful blue eyes glazed with sensuality, the sweet breath that escaped her parted lips, the pulse fluttering wildly in her throat, the rapid rise and fall of her chest. Smiling with satisfaction, he cupped the back of her head and ached with need when her eyelids drifted shut. He touched his mouth to hers again, making the contact more firm this time. Her lips were stiff and her body rigid with tension. It was as if she was unaccustomed to being in a man's arms, unused to the feel of his mouth against her own. But she'd once been engaged. How could this be?

Moving back a whisper, he ran the tip of his tongue across the seam of her lips, letting her know what he wanted. Her breathing grew more rapid, and she instinctively nestled her body closer, but her lips remained tightly pressed together. Did she not understand what he wanted from her? Could it be she was indeed as innocent as his aunt had suggested?

Penny jumped headfirst into the mind-blowing fire of Rafiq's kiss. The first touch of his lips to hers shut down her willpower and closed off coherent thought. New, unfamiliar sensations swept over her. Warmth spread from the soles of her feet to the roots of her hair, heating delicious, feminine places in between. Her breathing grew labored, as if she'd been his star pupil and raced her horse across the desert. How she longed for him to instruct her in the same precise detail about all things sensual. Wonder filled her to overflowing and with a desperation she hadn't believed herself capable, she wanted him to touch her as if she were just like any other woman to whom he was attracted.

He lifted his mouth from hers. "Penny?"

"Hmm?" she answered without opening her eyes.

"Open your mouth for me."

Her eyelids popped open. "Oh, my gosh—"

"Do not be alarmed. I will educate you in this matter, just as I did with riding the horse."

She stepped away from him. "I'm completely mortified. I have to go back now."

"But—"

She turned away. "It's time to go. Don't you think it's time to go?"

Way past time. If only she'd hightailed it out of there five minutes earlier, she would have bypassed this quicksand of humiliation. Mercy kiss for the ugly duckling *and* she'd done it wrong. How horrible was this? Why would he do this to her?

"Penny—"

She whirled around. "Look, if you must know I haven't kissed very many men. In fact, none."

"But what about the jackal you were engaged to?"

"How did you know about that?" But she knew. There was only one person in the royal family she'd confided in. "Princess Farrah."

"Yes."

He stood there looking at her expectantly, and somehow she knew they weren't going anywhere until she explained the most degrading thing of all. If he weren't the ruler of this country, she would tell him what he could do and where to go do it.

Then she saw pity steal into his eyes. It was too much. He could stand there and wait till it snowed in hell for all she cared. No way would she bare her soul. She turned on her heel and walked over to her horse, fortunately remembering to untie the reins before mounting up. The speed with which she accomplished the feat convinced her Rafiq was a very good teacher indeed. Heat flooded her cheeks at the thought of him instructing her in kissing. She felt like such a fool. Pulling the reins to the right, she turned her horse and headed back in the direction from which she'd come. Tears blurred her eyes and she dashed them away, only then remembering Rafiq had her glasses.

Glancing over her shoulder, she saw him leap onto his horse, then look behind him and pull something out of his pocket. She sighed. When it went bad, it all went bad.

He nudged his mount and the animal sprang forward, falling into step beside her. Reaching out, he handed her the spectacles, snapped in two at the nose rest.

"I forgot about them," he said. "I will replace your glasses."

"Thank you." Her gaze slid sideways and she was thankful he was looking straight ahead. "And I don't ever again want to talk about anything not work related."

"As you wish."

Nothing was as she wished. She *wished* her life was simple. She wished she'd had more time with her mother. She wished she hadn't been so stupid and given her money to a man who had used her. She almost wished Rafiq hadn't kissed her. But none of her wishes had come true. Obviously her fairy godmother was a slacker.

Penny missed her glasses desperately as she struggled to read paperwork she'd brought home to look over. When a knock sounded, she was more than happy to turn her back on the blurred pages.

She answered the door to Crystal Rawlins. "Hey."

The nanny held out a roll of tape. "Hi. I thought this might help until you can get your glasses replaced."

"Thanks." Penny took the adhesive and opened the door wide. "Want to come in?"

Crystal hesitated only a moment. "Yeah. Fariq is spending some time with the children, and I could use a break."

Penny grabbed the two halves of her glasses before following the other woman into the suite's living room. They sat at a right angle to each other on the impressive corner sofa.

"How do you like caring for Prince Fariq's children?" Penny asked.

"I think it's the easiest—and hardest—job I've ever done. Pretty much what my mother always says about motherhood. I'm the youngest of six children," she confided.

"You're lucky. I'm an only child." She taped her glasses together and put them on. "There. It's nice to be able to see again. I'm afraid of passing King Gamil or Princess Farrah and saying nothing because I can't see who they are."

"Have you ever thought about contacts?" Crystal asked, pushing her own glasses more securely on her nose.

"I tried them once—unsuccessfully. At the time I was getting very little sleep what with working, classes and studying. I felt like I had every last grain of sand from the desert of El Zafir in my eyes. They watered all the time. It was awful. Specs are easier, cheaper and more efficient."

Her only mistake was letting a handsome prince remove them and kiss her. If only the sensation of his mouth on hers hadn't been so wonderful. She wanted to hate him for the subsequent humiliation, but it wasn't his fault. She was the dweeb who'd never been kissed. Glancing at her friend, she was tempted to confide what happened but decided against it. She'd had about all the embarrassment she could stand for one day.

"Your mind is made up?" Crystal leaned forward, serious concentration etched on her face.

She wore an emerald-colored silk blouse under a loose, floral jumper of coordinating colors. The clingy material molded to her figure. Her mahogany hair was pulled away from her face and secured at her nape. The severe style made her eyes stand out. They were a striking green, almost the exact shade of her blouse and fringed by thick, sooty lashes.

"Contacts are not for me," Penny answered. "But you should try them. Your eyes are so beautiful. You shouldn't hide behind spectacles."

"Funny you should phrase it that way."

"Why?"

"No reason." Crystal shrugged, obviously uncomfortable.

"I didn't mean to invade sensitive territory. Goodness knows I have no basis for judging in the beauty department."

"Why do you say that?"

"Look at me. I have no illusions about my appearance," Penny said, waving her hand in a gesture that encompassed her from head to toe.

Crystal scrutinized her. "Right now I'd have to give you first prize for geek of the week. If you're going for nerd of the year, all you need is a pocket protector."

"Thanks for the moral support," Penny said wryly.

"I'm sorry. But friends don't lie to each other." She looked slightly uncomfortable when she said "lie."

"Are we friends?" Penny asked.

"I sure hope so," Crystal said fervently. "And from one friend to another, that tape has to go."

"I don't have a spare pair of glasses."

"How'd they get broken anyhow?"

Penny felt heat wash into her cheeks as she remembered the series of events leading to the disaster. "It's a long story. Suffice it to say it was a shattering experience, on many levels," she added.

"Since the palace rumor mill has it you went riding

with Prince Rafiq, is it too big a leap to assume he was somehow involved?''

"Yes. No. Actually, if you don't mind, I don't want to talk about it.''

"I'm sure he would be happy to replace your glasses.''

"He already offered.''

"Maybe he'll spring for contacts. Since you have a normal nine-to-five job now they might work for you.''

"It's nine-to-five, but I wouldn't, by any stretch of the imagination, call it normal.''

"I know what you mean.'' Crystal grinned, showing straight white teeth and a beautiful smile. "But that remark about no illusions regarding your appearance implies you think you're not attractive.''

"In life you play the hand you're dealt.'' She remembered saying the same thing to Rafiq. "At the risk of being the cliché queen—when life gives you lemons, make lemonade. We all need to lead with our strengths. I've learned mine is brains not beauty.''

"But we're women. There's a lovely invention called cosmetics.''

"I don't think that would help.''

"You're wrong. Along with a hairstyle, clothes and a makeover, you could be a knockout. You have tremendous raw material to work with.'' Crystal pointed to herself. "This is me. I saw you without your glasses and before the tape.''

Penny laughed. "If you're really my friend, I gotta tell you it's not nice to give a friend false hope.''

"I wouldn't do that.''

"I wish I could believe you. Even more, I wish I

was sophisticated. What I wouldn't give to be tall, statuesque and stunning."

"The kind of gal who could catch a prince's eye?" Crystal asked wryly.

"Oh, no," Penny assured her quickly. She'd already caught his attention and didn't that just complicate the heck out of her life. She so did not need the distraction or the ensuing disaster. She had to keep her eye on her goal, not one tall, dark, dashing prince. "Although I'll admit he's good-looking."

"Which *he* are we talking about? Rafiq, Fariq or Kamal? And the king is no slouch, either."

"Rafiq. He's like the guy in high school who made you want to get out of bed every morning and go to class. The guy who gave you a reason to be there day after day. But I'll never catch his eye. Not in a million years."

"Not even one hundred and one Arabian nights?"

Penny shook her head and smiled. "Nope."

"Well, I have to warn you 'pretty' has its own passel of problems."

"Like what? I can't imagine any situation where being beautiful would pose a difficulty."

"Then you should be in my shoes," Crystal mumbled.

"What? Why?"

"Never you mind. I'm just trying to say that there are things more important than looks to worry about."

Penny sighed. "I know you're right. And I'm so grateful for the opportunity to work here in El Zafir. But I can't help wishing I were slightly less plain." Which reminded her. "Speaking of plain, do you have any idea why plain was a qualification for the nanny job?"

"I do," Crystal nodded. "It's because of your prince."

"If you're referring to Rafiq, he's not my prince."

"I am talking about Rafiq, and I refuse to debate whether or not he's yours. Time will tell."

"What about him?" Penny felt as if she'd swallowed a stone, and it just hit the bottom of her stomach.

"Seems the last nanny fell in love with him and threw the household into a tizzy because she decided to wait in his bed."

"Well, I guess that's probably not the best way to get a positive employee evaluation, but—"

Crystal's eyes gleamed. "That's not all. She decided to take off all her clothes while she waited."

"Oh, my."

"No kidding. Apparently, it wasn't the first time a woman on staff in the palace succumbed to his princely charms. According to palace gossip, he doesn't bother with plain women, so King Gamil made that one of the nanny requirements in order to bring some peace into the household."

Penny's eyes grew wide. If that was true, why had he kissed *her*? Had she caught his eye?

"So has working for him been a problem?" Crystal asked.

Not until today. "No," Penny answered. "Although I'm not the kind of girl who sweeps men off their feet, I do appreciate the warning."

Crystal stood. "I better get back. It's bedtime."

"Thanks for the tape," she said, standing also.

Life would be so much easier if her job was dealing with children instead of one dashing, charming prince. His kiss had made her toes curl and was indirectly responsible for the trauma to her glasses. But he didn't have to do anything so overt to charm her. All he had to do was work in the same office and breathe the same air.

She opened the door to see her friend out. "I enjoyed talking with you. Let's do it again soon."

Crystal smiled. "Sounds wonderful. We'll have to take Prince Rafiq up on his offer to entertain the children for an afternoon so we can explore the city together."

"I'd like that. Have a nice evening," Penny said.

"You, too." Crystal waved, then rounded the corner.

Penny closed the door and leaned against it. "Not likely. I'll be lucky to sleep a wink."

Now she knew about Rafiq's reputation with women who were her exact opposite. No doubt Princess Farrah had hired her because her looks wouldn't attract him. After his kiss, she'd wondered if maybe…

Nope. Maybe wasn't in the cards for her. She had to forget everything else and focus. She needed her job in order to achieve her goal. Letting her crush go unchecked would be stupid, and she wasn't a stupid woman.

"The last thing I need is to disrupt the household and be dismissed."

For a fairy-tale time at the oasis she'd lost sight of her goal, but it wouldn't happen again. This was her life, and she'd dedicated herself to starting a preschool in honor of her mother. Nothing would stand in her way.

Not even a sheik who was too mesmerizing for her own good.

Obviously, she'd miscalculated. Spending time with him in the desert was *very* different from the office. So her path was clear. All work, no play. And definitely no more hanky-panky with Prince Rafiq Hassan.

Chapter Seven

Rafiq rounded the corner into his office and nearly jumped back when he saw Penny and her patched glasses. The sight brought him back to the previous day and what it had felt like to kiss her lush lips and feel her soft curves molded against him. He let out a long breath and ran his index finger around the starched collar of his dress shirt, vowing to turn down the air conditioner a degree—or ten.

Her long-sleeved, high-necked black dress was one he'd often seen her wear. She was still not attiring herself in the new things. He'd been out of the palace on appointments that morning in preparation for the upcoming charity event still several weeks away. After yesterday, he decided not to bring up the matter of clothing. She'd asked to speak only of work. Technically, attire was fair game, but he didn't need a reminder of how lovely her skin looked in black lace.

It was time for the noon meal and, instead of getting lunch at one of the exclusive restaurants in the capital city, he'd felt compelled to come back to his office. He wasn't certain, but if he had to guess, he would say the lure was his quite original and very diverting assistant.

"Good day," he said to her.

She glanced up and did a double take. Obviously, she'd been absorbed in her work. It seemed to take her a moment to focus. Or did the broken glasses just make it look that way? He was responsible and would take pains to repair them.

"Rafiq. Good afternoon. I thought you wouldn't be back until after lunch."

"Have you eaten yet?"

She shook her head. "I was going to finish typing this report first."

Was it his imagination or was there pink in her cheeks and did it have anything to do with his kiss in the desert?

"I will have something brought in," he said.

"As you wish." She looked back at her monitor.

He walked past her desk, into his own office and picked up the phone. After giving his requests to the chef, he glanced through his messages, all written in his assistant's neat, legible script. So like her: small, precise, intriguing. What was wrong with him? Even when he tried to work she distracted him. It would end now. He was Prince Rafiq Hassan and a woman with large, ugly glasses was not enough to make him lose his considerable concentration. But in the next instant he picked up his phone and dialed his personal physician. A prince of the royal blood kept his promises.

A short time later lunch arrived and was set out on a cloth-covered table in the outer office where he joined Penny. When she looked up, the soft lines of her body tensed. Her full lips thinned to a straight line. It wasn't his imagination. She was indeed stiff and standoffish. As much as he'd jested about cutting out her tongue, he found he missed her ingenuous chatter.

"Let us eat," he said.

"As you wish."

The cloying phrase was beginning to grate on him. He held her chair and noticed she kept herself tense, giving him a wide berth to avoid their touching. Disappointment settled over him. He very much enjoyed touching her.

Rafiq settled her then rounded the table and sat across from her as the steward filled their plates with food. When the servent finished, Rafiq said, "I require nothing else. You may take your leave."

The young man bowed. "As you wish, Your Highness."

There was that cloying phrase again. Maybe it grated when Penny used it because he didn't think of her as an employee. He wasn't certain when that had changed.

When they were alone, Rafiq glanced across the table at his clearly uncomfortable companion. This monosyllabic, acquiescing Penny was unnatural. He wanted the woman he'd shared his oasis with. A woman full of laughter and warmth, the way she was before he'd kissed her. Although, even if he could have arranged it, he would not wish to take it back. Chaste though it was, the touch of his lips to hers was burned forever into his memory.

All he needed was to charm her out of her pique. Then he could find out why she was piqued in the first place, since his experience with women told him she'd enjoyed the kiss as much as he had. He needed to draw her out with a subject about which she was passionate. And he knew just the thing.

"Tell me about your plans for your preschool," he said, choosing a subject he knew was close to her heart.

She hesitated only a moment before saying, "What do you want to know?"

"Start from the beginning. Why is it so important to you?"

"I believe I already explained."

"I think it's more than love of children and following in your mother's footsteps. I have never met a woman who would go to such lengths as you have to start a business."

"When you're right, you're right. It's more than a business. I made a vow to my mother when she was dying. I promised her I would do something to keep her memory alive. Something good. Something to give kids a positive start in life like she gave me. I didn't have her nearly long enough, but I wouldn't be where I am today without her guidance and guts. I'm going to start the Mary Elizabeth Doyle Early Childhood Development Center."

"I see." The words were inadequate to convey the depth of feeling her explanation evoked. Her mother must have been a remarkable woman to generate such devotion in a daughter.

"I'm going to apply for grant and scholarship money to help underprivileged children attend preschool. We need to close the gap between disadvantaged and middle-class kids so they can all hit the floor running when they start school. My experience working with you on the charity fund-raiser will be invaluable when I go home. I hope to collect money for programs to assist single moms who have to work and need a safe and intellectually stimulating place for their children.''

''Have you chosen a site for the center?''

''Yes.'' She spread the cloth napkin in her lap and nodded.

The expression in her eyes, so cool after passion for her cause faded, told him he still had a way to go to smooth her ruffled feathers. He willed himself to patience. ''Where?''

She met his gaze and nudged her drooping, uneven, taped glasses up. ''It's not far from where my mother taught school. A residential area but several miles from the business section of town.''

''So you have a building?''

''Not yet.''

''You have purchased the land?''

She met his gaze again. ''No.''

''Then how can you be certain it will be available when you return to Texas?''

''I can't. I'm hoping. If I'd had the money to buy it...''

''But you don't.'' And he knew why. His blood grew hot at the idea of this honest and honorable young woman deceived out of the money her mother had left her. ''Tell me about this jackal, the one who did this to you.''

''It's not my finest hour. I'd rather forget about it.''

''Might it be easier if you told me?''

''You already know.''

''I'd like to hear it from you.''

She slid him a skeptical look. ''Is that a royal decree?''

''I could make it one.'' His words brought the beginning of a sparkle to her eyes, giving him a great deal of satisfaction.

"The *jackal* lived in my apartment complex. It was my bad luck it happened to be next door. He claimed to be an attorney, but I found out later he was a flunky in the office with access to my file. He was good-looking and charming. I was alone...."

"Go on," he quietly encouraged when she hesitated.

She nodded. "He spent time with me and I thought it was because he genuinely cared. The attention went to my head, I guess, disconnecting my better judgment. When he asked me to marry him, I accepted. So when he offered to invest my inheritance and double it, I never questioned him. He told me I could realize my dream twice as quickly with his help."

"He didn't invest it," Rafiq said, anger coursing through him.

Her fork clattered forcefully against her plate. "He might have, but not for me," she said, her voice clipped, bitter. "I never saw him again."

"Did you notify law enforcement in your country?"

"Yes. But there wasn't much they could do. He was using a false name. And I gave him the money. There was nothing signed or violated. Except my trust."

"I see."

She leaned forward slightly, her blue eyes flashing. "I was a fool on so many levels." She hesitated, and he thought she would keep it to herself, but she continued. Apparently, she did need to release the feelings. "Wasn't it good fortune for a girl like me to find a man like him who was a perfect gentleman? I never questioned why he treated me like a sister."

"Why would you?" Rafiq pushed away the uncomfortable feeling when he remembered his own intention to treat her like a sister. And how that had not worked out.

"He never planned to marry me. He only wanted my money. The whole time he was sweet-talking me to get his hands on it, he never kissed me."

"Never?"

"On the cheek, the forehead. The way I've seen you kiss Johara. If only he'd been gay." Her gaze faltered then, and she looked at her plate of half-eaten food. "He didn't even want to sleep with me while he was stealing my money."

"In El Zafir we have punishment to fit such a heinous crime," he said.

"For not sleeping with me?"

On the contrary. For that he could reward the beast. "No. For taking money from an innocent woman. In this country the price would be swift and severe."

One corner of her mouth lifted. "Beheading? Cut out his tongue? Drawing and quartering in the town square?"

"All of the above," Rafiq informed her.

He was pleased he'd coaxed a smile from her. Although why it was so important was a very large mystery. He had an idea that would put the stars back in her eyes and her lovely smile permanently back on her face.

"I could buy the piece of land you require for your preschool."

She blinked. "Is this going to be another Paris moment?"

"How so?"

"I can't accept anything I haven't earned."

He nodded. "An admirable quality. I was thinking

more of an advance on your salary. Putting a deposit on the property and taking it out of your earnings.''

She was speechless for several moments and he knew he'd gotten her attention and perhaps avoided exploding the land mine he'd mistakenly stepped on—again.

"I'm going to trust you. Because I made a promise to my mother, and I don't want to take a chance that the land won't be there when I get home. As long as you give me your word that the cost will be taken out of my salary in installments.''

"You have my word that the property will be in your name when you need it." He would save the details of payment for another discussion.

"All right then. I accept your offer of assistance.''

"Excellent," he said, nodding. "I will make the necessary arrangements to acquire the property.''

"Thank you." She looked down at her linked fingers. "I don't mean to be difficult. It's just that I learned a lesson the hard way. I won't be so gullible or innocent again.''

Her vehemence got his attention. It bothered him that the swine had taken her innocence of spirit. But he couldn't regret that her chastity was intact.

"Purity is a jewel to be treasured, not something inconsequential to be squandered on the unappreciative," he told her. "You should be proud of saving yourself.''

"I would be. If I'd been tested. But he never tried anything. There was no character-building going on.''

If her untutored response to his kiss at the oasis hadn't convinced him, her response just now had. He'd never before met anyone who was incapable of falsehood. Not until Penny. Aunt Farrah was correct.

Penny Doyle was innocent and untouched.

The realization fired his blood as well as his need to protect her. And possess her? No. He'd been forbidden. But he was oddly uncomfortable with the combination of feelings. They inflamed instead of easing his fascination. He wanted to kiss her again and was never more grateful to have a table between them. He was an honorable man who had sworn not to hurt her or bring disgrace to the House of Hassan. In truth, the moment was not worth the subsequent scandal.

Passion and attraction would fade. They always did. No woman had ever truly engaged his heart.

Penny couldn't believe she'd just told Rafiq the most embarrassing, painful episode of her life. It was different from embarrassing and humiliating—as in the kiss she'd shared with him. But now it was way past time to return to an innocuous subject. Or at least turn the conversation away from herself.

"Let's talk about you. You obviously see how important my mother was to me. What about yours?"

"I never knew her. She died when I was but a babe, never recovered her health after childbirth." He sipped water from a crystal glass. "You are fortunate."

"When you put it like that, I suppose I am. I'm sorry, Rafiq."

He shook his head. "My father raised his sons to be men. Aunt Farrah filled in. I have not missed a woman's touch."

"That's for sure," she said. Darn she hated when stuff just popped out like that. "I mean, from what I read about you. It seems you've not been at a loss for female companionship."

"Do not believe everything you read."

"Okay. But your name is linked with a lot of

women. Beautiful women from all over the world. In fact, one article called you the world's most eligible bachelor sheik.''

She teased him, because the look in his dark eyes when he'd mentioned his mother had tugged at her heart. It was almost as if she could see the little boy he'd been, missing a mother's touch. His aunt wouldn't have been the same. Penny hadn't had her mother for long, but it was long enough to know what a motherless boy had missed.

She couldn't afford to see his vulnerable side. He wasn't a puppy who, with one hug, would follow her around for life. Going soft and gooey inside would not protect Little Red Ridinghood from the big bad wolf.

''I am an eligible bachelor. And a sheik.''

''Have you ever been engaged?''

''No.''

''Why? At least I was engaged to be married once. Even if the guy was a con man.''

''I have come close several times. But one woman is very much like the next. When I must choose an appropriate woman, I will do my duty—marry and produce children.''

''What if an appropriate woman says no?''

''Preposterous. Of course she wouldn't dream of refusing the honor of marriage to Rafiq Hassan, Prince of El Zafir.'' He grinned. ''And there is the fact that women find me—appealing,'' he said with a shrug.

''So you do nothing to encourage them?'' Was she flirting? Again? What was it about the man that brought out this side of her? It takes one to know one?

''Of course not.'' One corner of his mouth turned up. ''Has anyone ever told you your eyes are quite beautiful?''

Speaking of flirting… "Yeah. Right," she scoffed.

"I speak the truth, for I have seen the truth. When they are not hidden behind glasses, your eyes are bluer than the blue in a cloudless desert sky."

He'd taken her glasses off under that sky he just mentioned. He'd kissed her until her body went dewy and her toes curled. He'd made her want more than kisses. In fact, he was making her feel the same way right now. Lord, was it just her? Or was it hot in here? She was as hot as she'd been under that El Zafirian sun and now it was nowhere in sight.

"And it is my fault that they are broken."

"My eyes?" she asked breathlessly.

His white teeth flashed in a tilt-her-world smile. "Your glasses. I have made an appointment for you with the palace physician. He will assist you in replacing them." He pointed at her. "We will have no debate over the bill. It is to be sent to me. I am responsible. I will make amends."

"Okay."

Black eyebrows rose. "As easy as that?"

"When you're right, you're right."

"I am always right," he said, his eyes sparkling with mischief.

This was how she liked him best, teasing with a subtext of tenderness that battered at the wall around her heart. Then she reminded herself this was his stock-in-trade. He was a flirt who oozed charm the way Mount Etna oozed lava. She'd almost forgotten that, one magic afternoon on a desert oasis. She couldn't afford to forget again.

Opening her preschool had been a career and personal goal for as long as she could remember. She now officially added another personal goal to her list—do not, under any circumstances, make the same mistake twice. Rafiq Hassan was toying with her. What else could it be? She was so out of his league.

If only the memory of the kiss she'd shared with him weren't quite so sweet.

Chapter Eight

Penny thought Rafiq looked tired. She noticed him the moment he walked into the palace ballroom. The breathtakingly beautiful palace party place had high ceilings, an expansive marble floor, numerous chandeliers polished to perfection and wall sconces filled with fresh flowers. Her boss was there to make sure everything fell into place for tomorrow evening's charity event. He looked like a general surveying his troops as he watched tables and chairs being carried in and arranged according to the diagram they'd worked out together.

Exquisite linens were stacked and ready to drape the tables. Food and drink had arrived along with a chef imported from New York especially to oversee the preparations for this special occasion. Rafiq talked to her about the menu and whether or not it would put the guests in a generous mood. If the food didn't, surely the expensive champagne and sumptuous dessert would.

Rafiq could have delegated supervision to someone else, but he wouldn't hear of it. Everything had to be perfect. He'd been working eighteen-hour days to make it so. To make certain El Zafir acquitted itself well in the eyes of the world. She'd been burning the candle at both ends as well. And it had nothing to do with the upcoming event and everything to do with the hunk handling the upcoming event. When he spotted her and smiled, her heart grew wings and felt as if it would fly from her chest.

He walked across the large room, agilely dodging deliverymen, and stopped beside her, by the wall and out of the way. "I like the clipboard," he said, nodding at her hands.

"Tease if you want, but I'm a list person and this helps me check things off. It makes me feel productive."

"Would I tease you?"

"In a hot minute."

Speaking of hot… The way he looked at her shot her body temperature sky-high, like the Texas heat index in August. It happened every time she was near him. She could only hope the king returned Rafiq's assistant soon so Penny could go to work for Princess Farrah as originally planned. Otherwise, her brain would be fried, like the rest of her.

"I want to thank you for your assistance in preparation for tomorrow evening," he said.

"You're welcome. Although I was hoping for something more along the lines of you couldn't have done it without me."

"But that would be untruthful. I could have done it." One eyebrow lifted even as the corners of his wonderful mouth curved up. His teasing expression.

"But having your help made the task easier and far more enjoyable."

He knew just what to say. No wonder he was in charge of foreign and domestic affairs. She could have an affair... No. She wasn't going there and would nip the thought in the bud.

"I hope everything goes off without a hitch," she said.

"As do I."

"Why is it so important to you?"

Penny already knew. She remembered what he'd said at the family dinner, shortly after her arrival in the country. But he was so passionate about something so worthy. The fire in his eyes and earnestness in his manner when he spoke of his cause made him so handsome she couldn't stop herself from asking. Breathlessly she waited to hear him tell her again.

His playful expression disappeared. "Hunger in the world is inexcusable. With resources, money and manpower it can be conquered."

"Wow," she said. It was all she could manage.

Rafiq was most impressive when he was passionate. But the incident at the oasis had given her personal experience with the business end of his passion. If she knew what was good for her she would forget the incident. She knew what was good, and unfortunately she couldn't forget. Nor could she prevent herself asking another question about his motivation. "If anyone understands why this is so important, it's me."

His eyes gleamed with the force of his emotion. "So you can also understand why I want to exceed every donation record ever set for this annual charity event. There is no reason why hunger, especially in children, cannot be eradicated. And it will be. The effects of long-term deprivation are severe. Stress, illness, irritability, an inability to learn. If we are to improve the world, we must start with children.''

"Hey," she said, lifting up her hand, clipboard and all, to ward him off. "I'm on your side. But you were probably just warming up for tomorrow night."

He looked sheepish. Or at least as sheepish as a sheik could look. "As you say—a dry run."

"Does your dedication have anything to do with your niece and nephew?"

"Fortunately, they have never been deprived of anything. But yes. I have traveled the world and seen many things, not all of it good. I have imagined how awful it would be to love a child as I do Hana and Nuri and be helpless to give them even a crust of bread or a sip of milk to ease their hunger."

"Heartbreaking," she agreed.

When he stared at her the depth of emotion in his black eyes was bottomless. "When the last hungry child cries for a crust of bread and is satisfied, I will be finished. And not before."

How wonderful was that? How compelling was he? As Penny looked into his eyes, she knew how easy it would be to fall in and drown. Not even a life jacket could save her if she didn't quickly get a grip on herself.

"Well," she said a bit breathlessly, "Obviously, you like children."

"Obviously." He grinned. "I like them very much."

"Then one wonders why you don't have any children of your own."

"One would be overstepping one's bounds by asking."

"From the time one arrived in El Zafir one has overstepped one's bounds boundlessly and lived to tell about it. Why shouldn't one take advantage of your fatigue and ask?"

She was tired, too. That was the only explanation she could come up with for her boldness. It was stupid to push. She'd done her level best to keep her distance since the day on the oasis when he'd kissed her. But for some reason she was too weary to puzzle out, his answer about why he had no children was very important to her.

"So, you are not above taking advantage of me?" He waved her off when she started to say something. "No matter. There's a simple explanation for my lack of children. I'm not married."

"Simple?" She couldn't stop it when a derisive sound slipped from her throat. "There's nothing simple about you."

"Indeed?"

"Is it possible your standards are a tad high?"

"They must be high. I am a member of the royal family of El Zafir. And I will marry one day."

"Not at the rate you're going. I just don't see that it's such a difficult thing to do."

"You have had so much experience?"

"Well, no. Let me clarify. It shouldn't be difficult for you. You've had numerous opportunities. What's the problem?"

"There is no problem. I have known many women and been attracted to some. In fact I have come perilously close to marriage." He shrugged as if that answered the question adequately.

He would be wrong. "Then what?"

"The attraction fades."

"So you cast the woman aside?" she asked, only half teasing.

"On the contrary." He straightened to his full six-foot-two-inch height, and every scrumptious inch screamed prince of the royal blood. "I wouldn't phrase it quite that way. But for her sake, as well as mine, when the fascination cooled, I extricated myself in the nick of time."

"Avoiding marriage?"

"While there was still an opportunity to salvage a friendship. I've been told I'm the family charmer. Whether or not it's true, I've been successful at maintaining a warm and friendly acquaintance with all the women in my life. I do not avoid my duty. As I said, when I am ready, I will marry."

She remembered. An appropriate woman. Penny felt as if a white-hot poker had gone straight through her heart. For a moment she forgot that he'd completely omitted the subject of love. She was far too jealous to think straight. He didn't deny that there had been many women; he was proud of the fact that they were all still speaking to him. And she hated it. How rational was that? About as rational as love. Which reminded her...

"Could it be you're afraid of love?"

"I am afraid of nothing," he said vehemently.

Could it be she'd struck a nerve? The look on his face told her he had one nerve left and she was getting on it. Time to change the subject.

Penny leaned against the wall and adjusted her new glasses more securely on her nose. She pressed the clipboard to her chest to hide her pounding heart, just in case he could see.

"There will be many women at the charity ball,"

she said with what she hoped was the right amount of casualness.

"Yes. I plan to charm them out of very large donations for a very worthy cause."

"You're just the man to do it. *And* stay friends. Isn't it a lucky thing that you're in charge of this formal shindig?"

Rafiq thought her tone a bit brusque but could find no cause for it. And no reason why the stars in her eyes should dim, but they did. Since when did he spend so much time analyzing the mood of his assistants? Since the moment he'd seen this one sleeping in his office

A Penny for his thoughts.

Surely there was some reasonable explanation for his behavior. He'd come to rely on her in the three months since she'd arrived. She'd become very good at her job, anticipating his wishes almost before he voiced them. He'd been only partly truthful when he'd said her presence had made the job more enjoyable. That part had been the truth. He wasn't sure he could have pulled it off with someone less efficient than Penny.

"Is there something wrong?" he asked.

"No."

She was lying. If he'd learned one thing about his garrulous American assistant, it was that Penny never used one word when twenty-five could better complicate an issue. How odd that he could read her like a book. As he'd told her, he'd known many women, but not one had prepared him for her.

He narrowed his gaze and folded his arms over his chest. "Tell me what is bothering you."

"If you insist. I don't think I should go to the ball.

I know you're concerned about putting on a perfect show because the rest of the world will be watching. What if I spill something? Or slip on the polished marble floor? Or use the wrong fork at dinner? What will the world say about a royal family who would hire such a klutzy assistant for their prince?''

Rafiq suspected there was more to her reluctance than she claimed. The stars in her eyes had dimmed when he'd confessed his intention to charm money from rich women. Is that what bothered her? Was the idea of his attention to other women disagreeable to her? He liked that. He would make sure she knew his behavior was for the greater good. Because her absence was not an option.

"Do not be afraid."

"Just like that? You order me not to be afraid and expect it to be so?"

"Yes."

"Wow. Pretty impressive. Can you order the nerves in my stomach to relax so I don't throw up?"

"Yes," he said, and smiled.

Slowly, and against her wishes, he thought, her mouth curved into a smile. "You're teasing."

"Yes. But make no mistake. This is an order. I require your presence tomorrow evening."

He walked past her and into the hall. Rafiq wasn't sure why, but it was important to him that Penny attend the event. He couldn't imagine going through the motions without her there.

In her robe, Penny sat on the padded stool in front of her dressing table while Crystal stood behind her, surveying the magnitude of the job in the mirror. Survey was a good word. It implied a lot of work with overtones of engineering to transform her into something the royal family of El Zafir could be proud of. Crystal had had the charitable but misguided notion of helping with Penny's hair and makeup for the charity ball.

Tonight was the night. The royal family was putting their country, not to mention employees, on parade for the world. The press corps would be out in force and the thought of it made Penny want to throw up. And she was pretty sure even an order from Rafiq wouldn't make that feeling disappear.

"Let's start with your hair," Crystal said, tapping her lip.

"It's long, straight and fine. Your worst nightmare. There's not a lot you can do. I'll just put it in a bun."

"You have the most awesome hair, the kind most men would give anything to run their hands through."

Penny shivered at the thought. Would Rafiq agree? But he wasn't most men. He was a prince; she was a pauper. 'Nuff said.

"I'm not the kind of girl most men, or any men for that matter, would want to get that close to." Although Penny still didn't understand why Rafiq had gotten close enough to kiss her. In spite of his admirable championing of children, the fact remained that he had a reputation with women. She wouldn't be gullible again.

"It could use a trim and shaping," Crystal was saying, as she brushed the waist-length strands. "But we don't have time for that. Not to mention it's beyond my sphere of expertise. Besides, you don't want me within cutting distance of your hair with a pair of scissors. No, we'll put it up all right, but not in a bun."

Penny watched, grateful to distract herself from the

butterflies in her stomach. In very short order, her hair was piled at her crown in a sleek, sophisticated style while artfully placed wisps framed her face. The arrangement gave her some height, which she desperately needed, not to mention the illusion of making her neck appear longer. Who knew a curling iron was, in fact, a magic wand?

"Wow."

"Yeah," Crystal agreed. "I'm good."

"Yes, you are. Okay, I guess it's time to put my dress on."

"Not so fast. I've got my cosmetic bag with me. I'm going to make a painted lady of you. Turn around and close your eyes."

"Why? Will I scream and jump back when I look at what you've done to me?"

"You're going to be gorgeous. Quit being so negative."

Though she was slightly miffed because she'd always thought of herself as a glass-is-half-full kind of person, Penny did as ordered. She let her eyelids drift shut as she sat with her back to the mirror. Her friend's hands moved over her face as she explained each application: first moisturizer, foundation, powder, then blush.

"Now for the window to your soul," Crystal said. "When I get through with you, you're going to voluntarily leave your four-eyes image behind, even at the risk of passing your best friend without recognizing them."

"I'm wearing contacts," Penny confided.

"Really? When did this happen?" her friend asked, as she carefully applied shadow and gently blended.

"Rafiq recommended me to his personal physician,

who sent me to an ophthalmologist for my new glasses. After an exam the doctor explained that there have been advances in contact lens technology since I last tried them and an experience now might be more successful. So I went for it. They weren't terribly expensive. I've been practicing with them and my vision is actually better.''

''Excellent.''

Crystal worked a while longer and finally said, ''Okay. Open your eyes. It's time for the coup de grace. Lipstick. Pucker up those pouty lips.'' After applying it, she instructed, ''Now blend and blot.'' She moved her lips back and forth to demonstrate and handed over a tissue. Penny kissed the tissue then turned toward the mirror. She leaned closer.

The woman looking back was…pretty. Shadow, liner and mascara made her blue eyes appear bigger and bluer, and a bit mysterious. Her skin was flawless, like porcelain, with artfully applied blush making her cheekbones prominent and picture perfect. She had pizazz with a capital *P*.

''Oh my,'' she said. ''Who is that woman and what have you done with Penny Doyle?''

''Am I an artist or what? Now let's get you into your party duds.''

The gown was hanging over her bedroom door in a garment bag. Crystal removed it from the protective covering and took the dress off the hanger, holding it for Penny to step into. She turned her back and let Crystal zip her. A déjà-vuish kind of shiver raced through Penny as she recalled the last time someone had zipped her dress. Not that she didn't like her friend, or appreciate her help, but when Rafiq had zipped her, the act had been almost a religious experience.

Pulling herself back to the present, she took her silver sandals from their box and stepped into them. Then she stood in front of the full-length mirrors that were the doors to her closet.

"Whoa," she said, turning to see herself from every angle.

Arms folded over her chest, Crystal stood behind her, smiling from ear to ear. "You look positively amazing."

"I don't look like myself, that's for sure."

The dress was long-sleeved and high-necked, falling to the floor in deference to conservative El Zafirian customs. Nothing like the little black number Rafiq had insisted on purchasing. But the flowing material was shot through with silver strands and sparkled as brightly as any of the palace chandeliers polished to perfection by bored-to-tears staff. She couldn't help wondering what Rafiq would say when he saw her.

"Do you think the royal family will be pleased?" she asked.

Crystal pushed her glasses up on her nose. "I'm going to go out on a limb here and translate 'royal family' to mean Prince Rafiq. Yes, I think you'll knock his sovereign socks off. And then some," she said under her breath.

"Good."

"Look, Penny, I know I've teased you about having a crush on Rafiq. And it could be interpreted as encouraging you—romantically speaking. But since I feel like a fairy godmother, permit me a warning. Beware of handsome princes in tuxedos. I have to tell you—"

"I know what you're going to say," Penny interrupted. "Ordinary girls like me do not live happily ever after with sheiks from exotic countries."

"Actually, I was going to say girls like *us*," Crystal countered, her tone wry. "And—"

"And when the clock strikes the magic hour of midnight, I need to be outta there because he will still be out of my league and I will still be his assistant."

"Yeah. But also remember—"

Penny held up her hands. "I know. Tomorrow no one is going to knock on my door and ask me to try on the glass slipper as proof he's the love of my life."

Crystal shook her head. "It's like you can read my mind."

"Don't worry." She pointed to her reflection in the mirror. "There's a girl in a fabulous dress. I'm not sure where Penny Doyle is hiding and at the moment, I don't care. Thanks to you and Madame Gisele, and Rafiq for his awesome office supplies," she said, lifting the A-line skirt out to the side, then letting it float around her, "for the first time in my life I feel pretty. All I ask is one night. Tomorrow, I'll go back to being just plain Penny Doyle, realist extraordinaire."

Crystal draped her arm carefully around Penny's shoulders and gave her a squeeze. "You go, girl."

"Seriously, walking in Cinderella's glass slippers holds no appeal for me. I don't need the distraction."

"Why not?"

"My plan to open a preschool. Maybe a chain. I'd like to make it possible for all kids to start on an even playing field. If I can arrange for scholarships, I can help more kids."

"Good for you," Crystal approved.

"That's why I came to El Zafir. In the States, it

would have taken a lot longer to earn the start-up capital I need.''

''I know I just warned you about Prince Rafiq, but don't forget to have fun, too. Just don't make the mistake of falling for him.''

''I won't,'' Penny promised.

''Okay. My work here is done. Have a blast at the ball.''

Penny winced. ''Please don't use the words *blast* and *ball* in the same sentence when you're talking to me. I'll be ecstatic if I don't fall on my face.''

''Are you working?''

''Sort of. Everything is in place, but I'm coordinating activities with the equivalent of the maître d', sort of a headwaiter or majordomo. Rafiq and I have gone through every detail with Emil.''

''So you can relax and have a good time.''

''I can have a *time*. Relaxing is not a slam dunk.''

Crystal made a sign of the cross in front of Penny. ''Go my child. Fly. Be free. Let your heart be light with the carefree abandon of a thousand camels—or something like that.''

Penny laughed. ''I think the cosmetic fumes have gone to your head.''

''Break a leg,'' her friend added.

''Enough,'' Penny groaned as she walked over to the bed and picked up the small silver clutch purse that matched her shoes. ''I think I've had about all the good-luck wishes from you this poor old heart of mine can handle. I wish you were going with me.''

''I'm on duty with the children since Fariq will be at the ball in an official capacity. He's with Hana and Nuri now. They put up a fuss about being left out until I promised them a surprise.''

"You're quite the consummate fairy godmother."

"I do my best. Now go. Don't ruin your makeup by worrying. You look like a million bucks. Remember, no guts, no glory." Then Crystal looked at her seriously, all the teasing vanished. "I have a feeling tonight is going to change your life."

Penny couldn't say a word to that. Her chest tightened, and her throat felt as if it had swelled closed. Nerves were an amazing thing, she thought, to shut down her vocal cords. She nodded, squeezed her friend's hand and left her room.

She didn't want to change her life. If fairy godmothers were taking requests, she wished only to do Rafiq and the royal family proud.

Chapter Nine

Rafiq stared at the vision in the doorway. Penny had entered the ballroom as it was beginning to fill with guests for the cocktail hour. After dinner there would be dancing and the charity auction, to bid for the donated items his resourceful assistant had secured. All in all, he had a good feeling about the event's outcome. Between contributions already accepted and the minimum rather pricey donation for attending the socially prominent event they would raise a worthy sum. And Penny's assistance had been invaluable.

He'd known the instant she'd arrived, as if his masculine radar was finely tuned to her feminine frequency. The enchantress standing so nervously just inside the room was indeed Penny Doyle, but this moment she looked like a princess.

She took his breath away.

His heart had stuttered at the sight of her and now pounded like a horse's hooves racing across the desert. He started toward her then felt his arm seized.

"Your Highness."

Reluctantly Rafiq stopped and looked down at the woman. "Good evening."

"Nice party."

"I'm glad you're enjoying yourself."

"You don't remember me, do you?" she asked.

Rafiq studied her—brown hair, hazel eyes, full lips, tall. She was attractive enough, he supposed. But she was correct. He did not recognize her. "I beg your forgiveness, Miss…"

"Amanda Arbrook. We met last year at an event in London."

"It is indeed a pleasure to see you again, Miss Arbrook."

He remembered the name. Her father was a wealthy American who'd made a fortune in computer technology. Rafiq was counting on a large donation from him. He glanced across the room and noticed Penny was smiling and talking to a man only several years older than herself. Tension coiled inside him as a red haze blurred his vision. His breathing grew labored, as if he'd run a long way.

"Please call me Amanda."

He struggled to concentrate. "And you must call me Rafiq."

"I'm very excited to be here tonight. This is such a worthy cause."

"Indeed it is," he said, looking over her right shoulder to keep an eye on Penny.

"Daddy already gave your father a rather large check."

Rafiq bowed. "My thanks to your family."

"It's the least we can do. I was hoping you and I could get reacquainted."

"I would like that as well. Please, save a few moments for me later. Right now there's someone I must speak to if this evening is going to be a rousing success. Will you excuse me?"

"Of course," she said graciously.

He bowed again, then continued across the room where Penny now stood by herself.

"Rafiq, I—"

"Who were you talking to?" he demanded.

"When?"

"Just now. From across the room I saw another man speaking with you. I didn't recognize him."

"Oh." She smiled and the radiance was dazzling. "That was Peter Michaels, from England. He's in telecommunications and donated a tidy little sum."

"What did he say to you?"

She looked puzzled. "That he donated a tidy little sum."

"Nothing else?"

"Small talk. What else would he say? We're here for charity."

"Not everyone," he said, scanning the room. "Some would take advantage of this gathering."

"Take advantage how?" she asked.

Obviously, she was too innocent to recognize a wolf on the hunt. The idea of Penny as a man's prey stirred the embers of his anger. "Never mind."

She looked up at him and smiled. "You clean up real nice."

"Does that mean you approve of my attire?" he asked, one corner of his mouth lifting. For reasons he did not understand, he could never stay irritated at anything or anyone very long when Penny was nearby.

"I give that tux two thumbs up."

"Though I'm not a cowboy, you think I'm handsome?"

"I thought we agreed it's time to let that go." Her mouth thinned and she shook her head. But the twinkle in her blue eyes revealed that she was anything but annoyed with him. "I can't believe you're fishing for a compliment—from me of all people."

"Yet I am," he admitted. "So?"

"So, you know you look good."

The fact that she found him handsome at the same time she could take him to task for his behavior was exhilarating. He noticed the pulse at the base of her neck fluttered wildly. Was it his nearness? He hoped that was so, but asked, "Are you nervous?"

"Not really," she answered, looking up at him.

Her eyes appeared large and exotic. He suddenly realized she wasn't wearing the huge, hideous broken glasses. Or the improved but still concealing replacement glasses. "Are you able to see? Perhaps you need assistance?" He held out his arm.

She lifted her hand, then hesitated and met his gaze. "Why would I need help?"

"I will see that no harm comes to you," he explained. "You do not trust me?"

"It's not that. I was just trying to decide whether or not to come clean."

"Come clean?"

"I'm wearing contacts. I can see better than ever."

"That is good."

Ha! Just his luck. He'd sent her to the physician who improved her vision without glasses and she wasn't nervous. He could think of no excuse to stay by her side except that he wanted to be there more than any other place on earth. Straightening to his full height, he decided he didn't need an excuse. He was Rafiq Hassan, a prince of the royal blood. Tonight he would damn well make sure jackals on the prowl kept their distance from his innocent lamb.

"I should go check with Emil and make sure everything is running smoothly," she said.

Just then the orchestra began a lovely, sweet waltz, giving Rafiq a reason to keep her there. "Right on schedule. Obviously, Emil has everything under control." He held out his arm again. "Would you care to dance?"

"I don't know. I hate to monopolize you. Don't you have to go charm women? Out of their money, I mean?"

"There's plenty of time for that," he said, unwilling to leave her side, yet not at all clear about why that was so.

"Is it proper for you to dance with me?"

"Not only proper, but necessary."

"How's that?" she asked, slanting a suspicious look up at him.

"Duty dictates we demonstrate that it is permissible for our guests to dance. After all, guests having a good time are more likely to be generous. Especially when the combined wealth in this room could finance a small land war for an indefinite period of time. We, however, would like them to donate to a much worthier cause."

"I never thought of it like that." Penny placed her hand in the bend of his elbow. "Far be it from me to shirk duty."

"A woman after my own heart."

Rafiq realized it was true. She was a vibrant, exhilarating woman who met each challenge with courage, common sense and good humor. Tonight, she was completely stunning.

After leading her to the dancing area near the orchestra, he took her in his arms. Wishing they were anywhere but this very public ballroom, he glided into the steps of the waltz. She easily followed his lead. And why not? She looked like an angel. Of course she would float above the ground.

"So, what do you think of the dress?"

He glanced at her gown and decided this was not the time to be truthful. She looked lovely in the garment yet he wished she wore nothing at all. "I cannot tell you what I truly think."

"That bad?" she asked, her smile slipping.

"Not at all. It pales in comparison to the woman who is wearing it."

She smiled. "You are a silver-tongued devil."

"On the contrary, I speak the truth. You look beautiful."

"Is that what you really think?"

"Yes. I would not lie, not even to spare your feelings. My next thought is that I wish you were wearing the black dress."

Her steps faltered, and he tightened his arm around her waist, pulling her more tightly against his body. The sensation drove him wild, and he contemplated how he could unsettle her a second time, so that she would stumble charmingly into his arms again.

She slid her hand onto his shoulder. "You said that dress is too revealing. Remember? I told you it was a waste of money, and I would never wear it."

He let his gaze devour her lips. "Never say never," he said, then lowered his head and whispered in her ear. "I *will* see you in it again."

When he felt a hand on his arm, he straightened and stopped, nearly growling that he would allow no one to cut in.

"Good evening, Nephew. Penny." Aunt Farrah stood beside them.

"Your Highness," she said, nodding to the older woman. Penny stepped away from him. "You look wonderful tonight. Your gown is stunning."

His aunt wore a gold, formfitting garment with a high neck and long sleeves. For a woman her age, she looked exceptional. For a woman of any age, he amended, relieved he hadn't said anything so qualifying out loud.

"I am sorry to interrupt your dance. Rafiq, your father and brothers are waiting with your sister. Johara is tired and doesn't feel well. We would like to form a receiving line to greet our guests. Then she can retire."

Irritation shot through him as he was torn between duty and desire. "I will be there presently," he said finally.

"Very well. I will see you later, Penny?" the princess asked.

"I hope so," she answered sincerely.

Rafiq looked down, reluctant to leave her, knowing his absence would permit another man to approach her. The idea made him insane. And for the first time in his life, he felt vulnerable. He didn't quite understand how, but instinct told him there was potential for a great deal of pain where his assistant was concerned. Perhaps in the same way his father yearned still for his mother. Penny had asked him once if he was afraid of tender emotions for a woman. Was he? Surely not. He feared nothing. But he did not like this feeling. Or the idea that another person could impact his happiness for a lifetime. Somehow he must find a way to stop this weakness before it was too late.

Penny watched Rafiq whirl a tall, hazel-eyed American woman around the dance floor. She knew for a fact the woman's father had already given a generous donation to the fund, yet her boss was sparing no charm on Amanda Arbrook.

Jealousy licked through her, yet she had no right to feel it. He was a desert sheik; she was his girl Friday. Tell that to her inner child who wanted to pull the other woman's hair out. Trying to distract herself from the unproductive thoughts, she focused on the evening's events.

The ball had been a rousing success. Penny could hardly wait until the donations were tallied, expenditures deducted and they had a firm bottom line. Preliminary estimates indicated the silent auction proceeds were better than Rafiq had expected. The trips to a deserted island and a game preserve restored to its former natural state in Africa had fetched enormous bids. Other rare donated items had done well, too. Now the evening was winding down and only the hard-core revelers were left.

She wanted to go to her room to spare herself the sight of Rafiq charming other women. But she couldn't. It was part of her job to stay to the bitter end. She noticed Rafiq smile at the beautiful American who was everything she, Penny, was not. She turned from the sight and decided there was no El Zafirian policy against employees going outside for air.

She stepped through one of the ballroom's French doors and into the garden. The earthy scent of rich soil sweetened by jasmine tickled her nose along with other floral scents that blended into a fragrant, beguiling perfume. Subtle light illuminated the area and highlighted palm, date and willow trees and their artful arrangement. This part of the palace grounds was like a fairyland. And she felt like Cinderella. How appropriate. Though the sight of another woman in Rafiq's arms reminded her not to believe in fairy tales.

She wandered along the stone path to a fountain, brilliantly lit. The dancing water charmed her as the breeze blew across it, cooling her heated cheeks.

Heavy footsteps sounded behind her. "So this is where you ran off to."

She turned to the man. "Rafiq."

"You were expecting someone else?" The dark, smoldering expression in his eyes made her heart catch.

"You're neglecting your wealthy women."

He made a dismissive sound. "They are not my women. You are—" He stopped and intensity made the angles of his face harder, more sharp. "You need me."

"Really?" Her heart pounded as she tried to concentrate on breathing.

"It is my duty to stay by your side."

"How do you figure?"

"You look incredible tonight. Men will flock to you, to bask in your radiance. I, myself, am having difficulty resisting you. And I would kill any man who touches you."

"I don't think that's necessary," she said, barely suppressing the urge to bite her knuckle and restrain squeals of excitement gathering steam inside her. He was having trouble resisting her? He thought she would be attractive to other men? Could she believe that? It wasn't wise. "No one's going to touch me. I'm perfectly safe."

"Of course. I am here. If any man is tempted to seek you out, my presence will discourage him. Thus avoiding the scandal that would surely result if I had to defend your honor."

"I see. So spending time with me is all about protecting family and country. Simply a duty."

"Exactly," he said, his tone rife with satisfaction.

"And why would you think I might attract attention?" she couldn't help asking.

"Are *you* fishing for compliments?" He grinned suddenly, his teeth very white in the moonlight.

"Takes one to know one," she defended. "Seriously, I can't imagine that I would draw anyone's notice."

"You would be wrong. There is something different about you tonight. A confidence. A flirtatiousness I have not ever seen. My dear Penny, you are temptation personified. You are as intoxicating as expensive champagne."

She had to question his words. Her one and only experience with a man had been a disaster and her one and only kiss with Rafiq had proved she didn't know the first thing about it. How could he compare her to champagne? But offering to kill anyone who hurt her, that was pretty darned intoxicating. If only Rafiq had been around when her inheritance had been stolen. Her heart was pounding so hard her chest hurt, but in the most wonderful way possible. How in the world was she supposed to resist him?

Then common sense prevailed. Why would she have to? He was merely being polite. He felt respon-

sible for the innocent hick from Texas. Since that one
time in the desert, he'd shown no interest—correction—no *romantic* interest in her. Even if she couldn't
help falling for him, one-sided feelings weren't a
threat. It wouldn't sabotage her goal.

That decided, a question popped into her mind. She
tried to push it away, but the darn thing wouldn't
budge. So she decided to bring it out in the open.

"I can't help wondering," she said. "What would
compel you to kill a man on my behalf?"

Rafiq looked down at her and the intensity in his
expression stole the air from her lungs. His gaze
seemed to brand her with its heat. Without a word, he
slipped his arm around her waist, leisurely, deliber-
ately, relentlessly drawing her to him while his gaze
held hers captive.

"If a man was so bold as to do this, he would
deeply regret it."

Inch by unhurried inch, he lowered his head toward
her. Anticipation did battle with the nerves inside her
until she thought she would die—or run again. But she
desperately wanted to know how it felt to kiss Rafiq
correctly. She forced herself to wait, prepared to follow his lead, wherever he might take her.

Finally his mouth settled on hers. When he traced
the seam of her lips with his tongue, her heart thumped
against the wall of her chest. But this time she was
not quite so innocent, thanks to him. This time she
opened, and he didn't hesitate to take what she offered.
He delved inside, thrilling her with his possession as
he teased and caressed. Then he retreated, making her
sigh with regret.

He drew back slightly, compelling her to look at
him. The intensity in his expression took her breath

away. Then he cupped her cheek in his palm and her eyelids drifted shut as he bent toward her. He kissed her eyes, a touch as soft and gentle as the brush of a butterfly's wings. The next thing she knew, she felt his lips nibbling the corner of her mouth, her cheek, then a spot on her neck that sent tingles racing up and down her body.

Heat exploded through her, settling in her belly. Lower, in her most feminine place, something changed, as if readying for his ownership. Her breathing grew labored, leaving her dizzy and light-headed.

Then she felt the palm of his hand close over her breast. She hadn't thought she could feel more, but she was wrong. Her body seemed to take over, full steam ahead on basic biology. Her breast swelled and settled into his touch as if she were made just for him. Or was it because he was the only man who could bring out the woman in her? Her chest labored as her lungs struggled to move the air she needed to breathe.

Against her lips, he said, "If any man did this, he would *not* live to regret it."

"Oh, my—"

"You are a rare and precious jewel. I will be the one to teach you about all the pleasures awaiting you."

The blood rushed to her head, pounding in her ears. She thought she heard him say, "No other man will have you."

But then, he nestled her more securely in his arms and held her in the tenderest of embraces. Strangely enough, she felt as if he was protecting her from spies and bad guys and anything fate could throw at her. She never wanted this moment to end. He cupped her cheek in his warm palm and touched his lips gently to hers just before he took control and possessed her mouth with a thoroughness that kept her from thinking at all.

Warmth pooled in her belly and spread lower, sending liquid heat singing through her. She felt as if she'd been out in the sun too long, and her legs threatened to buckle. If he hadn't held her in his strong arms, surely she would have collapsed in a heap.

She couldn't shake the feeling that she'd been running all her life. Running and looking—for Rafiq Hassan. Now she'd found him and he was holding her and kissing her—eyelids, nose and jaw—on his way to her throat and a sensitive spot just beneath her ear. When he found it, she jumped as if touched by a live electrical wire. She'd found him and she never wanted to leave.

Just then voices drifted to them, and they jumped apart. She noticed Rafiq draw in a deep breath of air as he ran shaking fingers through his hair. Was he as aroused as she? That couldn't possibly be. A woman like her did not arouse a man like him.

Before she could puzzle over it further, Prince Kamal rounded the curve in the path and headed toward them. And he wasn't alone.

Penny had seen the woman earlier. She was quite pretty. The crown prince was pointing out the garden's sights to his companion when he saw them and smiled.

"So this is where you two disappeared. My brother Rafiq and his assistant Penny Doyle—a countrywoman of yours," he introduced them. "This is Alexandrite Matlock."

"Ali," the woman said holding her hand out first to Rafiq, then to Penny.

"Alexandrite?" Rafiq said. "Isn't that a jewel?"

"Since my parents have a sense of humor and saddled me with this name, I've done some research. Alexandrite comes from beryl, which is sometimes used
as a gem. But it's actually a hard mineral."

Kamal smiled down at his companion. "How appropriate. She is a hard woman."

Penny studied her. She wasn't tall. Her brown hair
was swept up into a simple loose-curled arrangement
at the crown of her head. Brown eyes the color of
whiskey were full of warmth and humor.

"I am not a hard woman," she countered. "I'm just
not susceptible to your flattery. Translation, I won't
give in to your request."

"It's not flattery. And I am merely attempting to
point out the finer points of El Zafir. I am very proud
of my country."

"As well you should be," Ali said.

"I feel as if we've come into the theater in the middle of the movie," Penny said.

"Forgive me," Kamal said. "Our aunt became ac-
quainted with Miss Matlock on her last trip to the
United States. Ali is a nurse. Princess Farrah offered
her a position in the hospital, which is now under construction in the city."

"Aunt Farrah should be the official minister of Hu-
man Resources in the country," Rafiq commented.
"She shows a remarkable talent for finding skilled
personnel." His eyes gleamed when he looked at Ali
and then his brother.

"Aunt Farrah invited Miss Matlock to the ball tonight, to give us the opportunity to—twist her arm, as
you Americans say. I have made her an offer I hope
she is unable to refuse. We would like her to accept

the director of nurses position in the women's wing of
the hospital.''

Ali laughed. ''It's tempting. A wonderful addition
to my résumé. And I'm impressed as well as charmed
by everything about El Zafir.''

''Then you must accept my offer,'' Kamal said.

''I don't think my fiancé would jump up and down
with joy if I took a job halfway around the world.''

''You are engaged to be married?'' Kamal looked
surprised.

''Yes.''

''El Zafir's loss is one lucky man's gain,'' Kamal
said. ''Still, I don't believe you're a woman who
would come all this way if the offer was out of the
question.''

''You think you know me that well, Your Highness?''

Penny wanted to pull her fellow countrywoman
aside and advise her to stay away from princes bearing
gifts. She touched her own kiss-swollen lips and
looked up at Rafiq. Thank goodness they'd been interrupted, preventing her from making an even bigger
fool of herself.

''I must go and see to things inside. If you'll excuse
me, Your Highness?'' Penny said.

''Of course,'' Kamal answered.

''Ali, it was nice to meet you.''

''And you,'' she said graciously.

Rafiq bowed to the woman. ''A pleasure for me
also, Miss Matlock. I will escort Penny—''

''No!'' She needed to escape from him, but hadn't
meant her tone to be so sharp. She looked at her three
surprised companions. ''I mean, don't let me interrupt.

Stay and visit. If the crown prince can't persuade Ali to accept the job offer, I feel sure Prince Rafiq can.''

Before anyone could say anything, Penny moved past the newcomers and hurried back into the palace. Rafiq had said he would protect her, but who would protect her from him? Once upon a time, she'd made a whopper of a mistake falling for a man who'd only wanted her money. But Rafiq already had more than she could even imagine.

So what was that kiss all about? What did he want from her? Why couldn't she resist him? Was she destined only to be attracted to inappropriate men? Was she grist for the talk-show mill—women who fall for men they know they can't have because they're really afraid to be happy? As she stepped through the French doors and back into the ballroom, she realized she'd done it yet again. She was in danger of falling for a man who was so far out of her league she would be an idiot to step up to bat.

A hysterical laugh bubbled up inside her as she thought of Cinderella losing her shoe while she raced from the palace. Penny was going in, but she was in danger of losing more than footwear. Her dress could turn to tatters, her coach to a pumpkin. And her hopes and dreams could go up in smoke.

Earlier, Penny had put into words what Crystal had been thinking. It was a sure bet Rafiq wasn't going to try a glass slipper on her dainty foot. Even if he did, it wouldn't fit. She didn't fit. Especially not in Rafiq's arms.

The last time she had fallen for a man—an ordinary man—a dream that had been within her grasp slipped from her fingers. She'd vowed never to be so foolish and stupid again. But the intensity of her feelings for

Rafiq frightened her. Experience had taught her to be wary. She had a suspicion this experience could be far worse.

This time she could lose everything—her heart and soul included.

Chapter Ten

Where was Penny?

Rafiq watched the path that led to the palace as he stroked his horse's nose. The animal snorted and shook his head, apparently sensing his master's restlessness. But damn it, she should have been here by now.

He had ordered their horses saddled and was now waiting in the pleasant early-morning spring air, just outside the stable. It had become their habit to ride in the morning before going to the office. He'd found the practice an agreeable way to start the day and feared it had more to do with spending time with Penny than stress management by physical exertion. Although he was especially eager for the exercise this day.

Why?

Did it have anything to do with the fact that the last time he'd seen her she'd been running from him? She had tried to hide it, but nonetheless she'd been fleeing.

Women did not run from Rafiq Hassan, they pursued him.

That in itself was disquieting, but he hadn't seen his intriguing assistant since the night of the charity ball. They hadn't worked over the weekend, and he'd been occupied with family matters and affairs of state. In spite of the beautiful day and the cooling breeze that carried the scent of the Arabian Sea, he was most impatient. She was late and this was out of character for her. His disquiet increased. Should he look for her?

He recalled the frightened expression in her eyes the night of the ball, before she'd scurried off, and was annoyed still that she had managed to escape. If his brother hadn't delayed him, he would have gone after her instantly. When he'd finally managed to excuse himself, he had been unable to find her.

Penny had been constantly in his thoughts—along with an eagerness to see her. This fierce need to possess a woman was completely foreign to him. Love? He snorted. When his horse tossed his head in response, Rafiq soothed the restless animal.

"It cannot be love, my friend," he said to the horse. But he remembered the question his aunt had asked the day Penny had arrived. Had he ever been in love? Was his education in that regard sadly lacking? "The emotion is nothing more than weakness, a word designed to make a man vulnerable. I am immune."

But he was not immune to jealousy, he thought. As a vision of Penny talking to another man filled his head, he fervently wished for exemption from that particular feeling. He didn't like it. Especially when her eager response to his own kiss told him that she craved his possession as much as he desired her.

He kept expecting the intensity to wane as it always did. Instead, the yearning grew stronger.

He didn't know whether to curse Kamal or thank him for the intrusion that had helped Rafiq keep his promise not to touch his innocent American assistant. But his honorable intentions were strained to the point of breaking.

"Where is she, my friend?" he said, patting the animal's nose again. "If she does not arrive soon, I *will* find her."

The next instant, Penny rounded the corner of the building, breathless, as if she'd hurried. "Hi," she said, not meeting his gaze.

"You are late."

"I'm sorry. I just came to tell you I can't ride."

"No matter," he said. "We can do it tomorrow."

"No. You go ahead. I meant *I* can't ride with you. Not anymore."

Annoyance and irritation twisted together inside him. He had the strangest feeling that she hadn't planned to come at all. But knowing Penny's penchant for fairness and honesty, she had arrived—late. "I have grown fond of our excursions. Is there a reason you can no longer accompany me?"

She walked over to her horse and stood with her back to Rafiq. She caressed the animal's nose and it appeared her hand was shaking. "No doubt you'll have your assistant back soon, and I'll be working for Princess Farrah. I won't have time. I will be learning different duties and will have to concentrate all my attention on that."

Annoyance and irritation coiled into anger. He willed himself to control this singular reaction. It wasn't that he was turned down by a woman. It was rejection from *this* woman. Because every last one of his male instincts said she wanted him.

"Liar," he said softly.

Her shoulders tensed, as if he had shouted the word, telling him he had guessed correctly. Why was she making excuses?

"I wasn't aware you had such a low opinion of me," she answered.

"Until this moment I thought quite highly of you."

"I'm sorry you don't understand. But I feel it's for the best." She started to walk away without looking at him.

Rafiq seized her upper arm to halt her and felt her trembling. His hold was gentle, but she would have to struggle for release. He did not plan to let her go until he received satisfactory responses to his questions. And reassure her she had nothing to fear from him. "Where are you going?"

"To the office."

"We are not finished discussing this." Standing behind her, he held her upper arms in his hands.

"There's nothing left to say."

"On the contrary, I have much that I want you to hear."

"It won't do any good."

"Are you afraid of me?" He turned her to see the expression on her face.

"I can't—" She shook her head. "Please let me go."

"Is it because I kissed you in the garden? Did you not like the way it made you feel?"

"Oh, no. I mean, yes. I've never felt like that before."

"Ah," he said, smiling with satisfaction. "So. You

are fearful of the new feelings that are so foreign to you.''

''It's not just that.'' Her glance darted everywhere as if searching for escape. Finally, she turned worried blue eyes up to his. ''It's so complicated. Please just let me go.''

He would give her almost anything. Anything except allowing her to leave him. As he gazed down at her, he desired to touch the seductive line of her throat, the intriguing curve of her delicate jaw, and he could only think about tasting her. He reached out a finger and tucked her hair behind her ear. She trembled at his slight touch.

Smiling with satisfaction, he lowered his head and touched his lips to the indentation where the column of her neck curved into the path of her shoulder. He heard her small gasp of pleasure and desire settled low in his belly. So, he hadn't been wrong. She was drawn to him, too. Which begged the question: Why was she trying to leave him?

Lifting slightly, he noticed that she'd let her head fall sideways, giving him free access to the soft perfection of her neck. And her eyes were closed, her lips parted slightly and her breathing accelerated. The sight of her—so innocent yet on the brink of wanton abandon—he knew he must have her.

Before he could act on the thought, footsteps sounded behind him. Turning, he saw his aunt Farrah in jodhpurs, knee-high boots and a white silk shirt. Obviously, she'd arrived for her morning ride. There was no mistaking the disapproving expression on her face. As a boy he'd been on the business end of that look. And his father's version of it.

''What is this, Rafiq?''

Penny tensed and took a step away from him, out of his grasp. "Princess Farrah!"

"Hello, Penny." Her eyes hardened when she looked at him again. "I see you've chosen to disregard my directive."

What could he say? He was caught red-handed, as the expression went. "There is something I must explain, Aunt. I have—"

She waved a hand in dismissal. "I am disappointed in you, Rafiq."

"But, Princess," Penny said. "Nothing happened. Really. I just came to explain to Rafiq why I can't ride with him anymore."

"Yes. I see how he seeks to change your mind," the older woman said. "I warned you, Nephew. But I suppose I should have known better. Grown men are like little boys. You all want what you are forbidden to have."

He straightened to his full height. "I am Prince Rafiq Hassan—"

"And I'm the woman who knew you when you were a baby—and then a little boy. Do you think I don't know what's going on here?"

He struggled to control his temper. "Yes. You have no idea what's going on."

"You are quite wrong, Nephew. I can only hope you will do the right thing."

Rafiq glanced to his left and saw the bewildered expression in Penny's eyes. Every instinct he possessed urged him to pull her into his arms. To comfort her. To explain—

What? Why?

"I will not stand here and defend myself." There was something quite important he needed to discuss with his assistant and he didn't want his aunt, or anyone else, present for the conversation. He nodded to them both. "There is business that needs my attention. Penny, I will speak to you later."

Penny's heart cracked. She watched the broad expanse of his back as he walked away. His stride was long and graceful. Yet there was the hint of a swagger and a suggestion of the predator. The thought sent shivers scampering over her body. Almost making her forget what his aunt had just said. Had she just been rescued from the clutches of the wolf?

"Your Highness, what did you mean about men being like little boys? Wanting what they're forbidden to have? Did you mean Rafiq?"

"Let me ask you something first. Did my nephew kiss you?"

"No." Penny crossed her fingers and put them behind her back.

The older woman's eyes narrowed. "So what I just saw was an illusion? Before you answer, I must tell you I have exceptional eyesight. This is the desert, but I don't believe I'm hallucinating. However, I could be wrong. It's been known to happen from time to time."

"Unlike other members of the royal family," Penny mumbled.

"So you're telling me Rafiq didn't kiss you?"

"He didn't." It wasn't quite an untruth since his lips didn't touch hers. He was on his way, but hadn't quite reached the mark when they were interrupted.

"Then answer me this," the princess said, her face taking on a shrewd, knowing look. "Excluding what just happened, has he *ever* kissed you? And don't even think about lying to me, Penny. I'll know if you do. It's one of the first things I noticed about you and one

of your best qualities. You couldn't tell a lie to save
your life.''

"What's the penalty in El Zafir for lying? Beheading? Tongue-ectomy? Dodging rocks in the town
square?''

"A lifetime of unhappiness," the princess said
gently.

And that was so much worse than anything she'd
said. "Yes, I've kissed him.''

"And did you initiate the kiss? Remember, don't
lie to me. Remove your hand from behind your back
and do uncross your fingers, child.''

Penny's shoulders slumped as tension slipped away.
Busted. Her only choice was to come clean. "Okay.
You win. Rafiq kissed me. But that's all—''

"And was it pleasant? Did you like kissing him?''
There was a tone in the woman's voice that sounded—
almost hopeful.

"It was—wonderful." Penny let out a long breath.
"But I don't understand what's wrong. What was he
forbidden to have?''

"You, my dear.''

"Me?" She pressed a hand to her chest, shaking
her head in confusion. "Now, I really don't understand. It's times like this when I miss my mother more
than ever.''

The princess moved in front of her and took her
hands. "It's not your fault. And I do hope you've
come to think of me as a sort of substitute for your
mother since your arrival in my country.''

"Yes." And Penny realized she had grown to rely
on the older woman as she hadn't on anyone else since
her own mother died. "But who forbade Rafiq to
kiss me?''

"I did. Just before he took you to Paris." She clucked sympathetically. "You are such an innocent. And I told him as much. That's the way you arrived in our country, and it is the way you will remain."

"Nothing happened between us, Your Highness. Honest. And I want to assure you it won't. I was just explaining to him that I can't ride with him again."

"Good." The princess patted her hand although Penny could swear disappointment dimmed her eyes and tightened her mouth. "I knew you were a level-headed young woman who would not be taken in by a handsome face and a glib tongue. Now, I think I'll go back to the palace."

"But, Your Highness, what about your ride?" Penny asked.

The princess glanced down at her attire. "I am no longer in the mood. Will you have lunch with me?"

"I would like that," she agreed.

"Good. Later, then."

Penny watched the second member of the Hassan royal family walk away. The whole scene was surreal and a vague feeling of disquiet settled heavily on her heart. One minute Rafiq had been kissing her neck, the next his aunt was reminding him he wasn't to touch the hired help.

Penny wondered if she was only a challenge to Rafiq, to see if he could seduce the virgin. Was his interest in her, his pursuit, his seduction merely the result of wanting what he was forbidden to have?

It made sense. He had more money than God. He could have any woman in the world, there was no way he would want her. Want maybe, but not love. At least not the till-death-do-us-part kind of love. But wouldn't it have been wonderful if she'd been wrong about the existence of modern-day fairy tales?

Chapter Eleven

Penny sat at the ornate desk in Princess Farrah's suite making schedule notes for the princess's day. She was off touring the new women's wing in the still-under-construction city hospital.

The phone rang and she answered, "Princess Farrah's suite, Penny Doyle speaking."

"I must talk to you. It's a matter of great importance."

Her heart pounded at the deep, seductive sound of Rafiq's voice. "You have your assistant back. I don't work for you any longer." Three agonizing days and counting. She missed him terribly and hated that she did.

"I am well aware that my aunt has appropriated your services. But it doesn't change the fact that I wish to speak with you."

"I'm very busy." She glanced at the too tidy desktop and sighed, mentally comparing it to her cluttered workspace in his office.

''You've been avoiding me.'' His tone was rife with accusation.

''I wasn't aware that you were looking for me.''

''You have not returned my calls and in your off time, you hide in your room. I have not seen you partaking in your customary pastimes.''

Did he even know what she liked to do when she wasn't working? She'd loved horseback riding, but that had more to do with the opportunity to spend time in Rafiq's company than anything else. In fact, what she liked most was working with him. But it was clear his aunt was displeased that he'd kissed her. That day, Rafiq's assistant had been released by the king, and Penny's services were required by the princess.

''Penny? Are you there?''

''Yes,'' she said, her fingers tightening on the receiver.

''I want you to have dinner with me this evening.''

''I can't.''

''Why?''

She was too scared. He was trying to seduce her, just to see if he could. And there was no doubt in her mind that he could. But *not* seeing him left a gaping hole in her life. She had a bad feeling she was in love with him and all he had to do was take one look at her face to know. She couldn't afford to be dismissed from her job. The only thing worse than being in love with a man she couldn't have was losing any chance of keeping her promise to her mother.

''I just can't,'' she said.

''That's not good enough. Tonight I wish you to have dinner with me. Seven o'clock. Wear the black dress.'' He paused for a moment. ''And, Penny, you may consider this a royal decree.''

Then the phone went dead.

*   *   *

Penny stood in the hall outside Rafiq's suite wondering what she was doing there. He was the last man on earth she wanted to see. And the only one she wanted to see. He didn't have to issue a royal decree. His voice on the phone had been deep and seductive. She could no more have refused than she could wave her magic wand and turn a camel into a limo.

As she brushed a hand down her thigh, she felt the knit material. It wasn't lace and she was covered from neck to ankle. He'd only said wear the black dress. But she remembered his face as he'd gazed at her in the Paris hotel mirror. No man had ever looked at her with such a dark, dangerous, passionate expression.

She yearned to see his face wear that intensity one last time. But that wasn't going to happen.

Okay. Here we go, she thought, raising her knuckles to his door. Two heartbeats later Rafiq opened it. Her first impression was that he'd dressed in a tuxedo. Then she realized it was a dark suit, with gray shirt and matching tone-on-tone tie. Regular business attire. Regular? She stifled a burst of laughter at the inane thought. There could never be anything regular about Rafiq Hassan. He was the most irregular, unusual, intriguing, dangerous man she'd ever met.

"Good evening, Penny."

She couldn't speak as his gaze raked over her from the top of her head to the tips of her black high-heeled shoes. It was a pair he'd purchased for her in Paris and she'd been unable to resist wearing them. The small amount of height gave her a bit more confidence—at least before he'd opened the door. Now her heart pounded and heat filled her cheeks, but she forced herself not to look away.

"You are not wearing the dress," he accused.

"It's black."

"So it is. And my mistake for not being more specific."

And then she saw it—the same expression she'd seen in Paris. She memorized the way his jaw clenched, making the muscle in his lean cheek jump. She imprinted in her mind his quick intake of breath at the sight of her. She learned by heart the way his eyes smoldered and seemed to catch fire as he took in each detail of her appearance. And she wasn't even wearing *the* dress. Was everything in her world out of whack?

He stepped back to allow her entrance. "Come in."

Said the spider to the fly.

"All right." Her heels clicked on the marble foyer floor.

She'd never been there before and had a first impression of endless space and exclusive—expensive—cherry-wood accent tables. Paintings adorned the walls and there were several exquisite crystal vases holding fresh bouquets of flowers.

He closed the door. "I wish you had worn the other dress."

"If wishes were horses, beggars would ride. I was just exercising free choice."

"Yes. Unfortunately, there is always a choice."

Not always, she thought. Not about falling in love with him.

"Not every woman can wear black as well as you do. You look wonderful. Although I do wish you had worn your hair down."

"I didn't get the memo." Had he missed her as much as she had him?

One corner of his chiseled mouth curved upward. "I will make sure you do next time."

There wasn't going to be a next time. But her heart ached at the thought.

"No matter," he said. "It's easily rectified."

He moved behind her and she noticed a large, beveled mirror reflecting the two of them. She watched him lift his hands and deftly remove the pins from her hair. The whole, heavy length slid down and shimmered around her face, falling over her breasts and shoulders. He reached around her and his fingers skimmed her breasts as he filled his hands with her hair, then lowered his head to breathe in the fragrance of the strands. The warmth of his body, the scent of his skin, the power of his presence combined to make her shiver. She was swiftly slipping under his spell.

"Such natural beauty," he said, trapping her hair as he curved his fingers into the palms of his hands. "A treasure beyond price."

She blinked, then took a deep, cleansing breath. Ooh, he was good. A silver-tongued devil—devil being the operative word.

She stepped forward, freeing herself from his grasp and her trance, then turned to face him. "What did you want to discuss with me?"

"You're in a hurry. Are you catching a plane?"

He didn't know how close to the mark he'd come. She'd seriously thought about it.

"Not exactly. I just want to get to the point of the evening."

"I will get to it. But first let us have champagne."

"Is there something to celebrate?"

The charity ball had been a success, but in the business wing of the palace they'd already nearly broken their arms patting everyone on the back. She was thinking like a peasant again. Expensive champagne didn't necessarily signal a celebration. The royal family probably drank it like water and for no special reason.

He took her hand and led her into his seductively lit living room. Candles were the only illumination, preventing her from seeing specific details. But there was a large white semicircular corner group sofa. In front of it, a silver bucket rested on a large glass-topped cherry-wood coffee table. He lifted the bottle and poured the golden liquid into two crystal flutes, then held one out to her.

"I wish to drink to us," he said.

Penny wondered if this was his best material, designed to make virgins putty in his hands. Or willing in his bed. If so, it was working, even though she knew what he was up to. Without the warning, she wasn't certain she could have resisted this long. In fact even with the heads-up, she wasn't sure she could uphold her resolve to keep him at arm's length. Case in point: her hair was down. He'd had to get in close to accomplish that. But she wouldn't let him near again.

She took the glass he held, careful to avoid his fingers. "Why don't we drink to guardian angels in high places?"

He frowned. "I do not understand."

"Do we have to drink to something?"

His eyes gleamed. "I wish to drink to you."

She took a healthy swig that lowered the amount in her flute by half. The way her hand shook, the less liquid in her glass the better. "What about me?"

"You are a most unusual woman."

"Thank you…I think."

She finished the rest of her drink while thinking that one over. It didn't sound like a traditional come-on line. Was he trying to confuse her?

"I meant it as a compliment." He refilled her glass, then sipped his own champagne. "You are smart, entertaining and capable of being trained. You learn fast and show the potential to be an asset to a man. You are sensible."

Where was he going with this? She studied him in the subdued light from the candles flickering around the room. His attire was impeccable. His jaw looked freshly shaven. In fact, she couldn't remember ever seeing stubble on his face. What was wrong with this picture? Ah, yes. He was male perfection; she aspired to mediocrity. And never the twain shall meet.

She felt light-headed and wondered if it was possible for the one drink to go to her head so fast. That was probably a yes since she hadn't eaten much of anything all day.

"Would you mind if I sat down?" she asked.

He bowed slightly. "Forgive me."

He set his drink down. Then taking her by the arms, he sat her down and she sank into the soft, cushy sofa.

She sighed. "Oh, that feels wonderful. You know, my feet were starting to hurt. I always wondered if sinfully expensive high heels would hurt less than the ones the average woman wears."

"And?" he asked, looking down at her.

"I saw the price tag on those shoes," she answered, hedging.

"Yes?" One dark eyebrow rose. "And?"

"They hurt just as bad," she confessed.

"I will speak to the designer."

Her eyes widened in surprise. "You can do that?"

"Of course."

Rafiq went down on one knee in front of her. Cupping her left heel in his large hand, he slid the shoe from her foot and set it on the coffee table.

"Wh-what are you doing?" she asked.

"Making you feel better."

"I feel fine."

The next thing she knew, he would be asking if she wanted to slip into something more comfortable. Even though men didn't hit on her personally, she'd seen it in the movies. She recognized a come-on when she saw one. Although his was different and a whole lot better than the jerk who'd taken her money. If she wasn't careful, he'd be unzipping her dress....

She recalled the heat when he'd zipped her up in Paris. Lord, if he made a move to bring her zipper down, she would spontaneously combust for sure. She'd let this go on long enough.

"Look, Your Worship—"

"You are angry?" he asked, frowning.

"What was your first clue?"

"Your form of address. You only use that one when you are less than pleased. I do not understand what is displeasing you."

"I'm on to you. Did you think I was so naive you could seduce me without so much as a by-your-leave?"

"What are you talking about?"

"Your aunt told me everything after you left the other morning."

"Define 'everything.'"

"She explained how she told you not to touch me

when you took me to Paris. She said men are like little boys, they always want what they're forbidden to have. And you know I'm—I never—I haven't—"

"Been with a man?"

"Yes. That." She let out a long breath. "Everything you've done—kissing me at the oasis, the expensive clothes and shoes," she said. "All that hooey the night of the ball, out in the garden, threatening to kill any man who touched me—"

The sob building momentum inside her forced her to stop and take a deep breath. How she'd wanted to believe he really and truly cared. How she'd yearned to belong, to a family—to something. To *someone*. And all the time he was probably laughing at her.

"You're as bad as the creep who pretended to love me and stole my money," she said. It was the worst thing she could think of. Apparently, it worked.

He surged to his feet and glared at her. "How can you insult me so? To compare me to that jackal—"

"If the shoe fits…" she said. "Not only that, you really need to work on your technique. What was all that stuff about me being unusual? Entertaining? Smart and capable of being trained?"

"I was getting to the part about being a good mother."

"What?" she asked, sitting forward so fast her fuzzy head began to swim. She put her full flute on the coffee table.

"And wife," he said.

"W-wife?"

"I wish you to marry me."

"What happened?" She snapped her fingers. "I know. The king told you it's time to choose an appropriate woman, I bet."

He shook his head. "No. It is my decision."

Stunned didn't begin to describe her feelings. Every girl dreamed of a proposal from a man. Some even dared to fantasize about the fairy-tale prince. She had done that when she was a little girl. But in her dreams and fantasies, the prospective prince usually declared undying love.

She swallowed the lump in her throat. "Forgive me if I missed the proposal. It sounded more like a job interview."

"And so it is. Wife to a sheik, prince of the House of Hassan, is a job in itself. It is my responsibility to choose wisely."

"Well, pardon me if I don't buy the act. I was fooled once by a good-looking game player. Don't get me wrong, you've got him beat by a country mile in looks, position and technique. But I'm not going for it."

"Going for it?"

"I don't buy the performance. It's ingenious. Propose marriage to a girl like me who would give almost anything to be part of a family. If I fall for it, you can get me in your bed and dump me in the morning."

"If you were a man, I would call you out for that," he said through clenched teeth. Then he tossed back the remaining contents of his champagne.

Penny knew she'd crossed the line. But she couldn't seem to slow down. She was dying inside and trying to get even. You always hurt the one you love.... How stupid was that? She'd actually fallen in love with him.

"If I were a man we wouldn't be having this conversation," she said.

She hoped with every fiber of her being that he would say he loved her. Apparently, her hopeless ro-

mantic streak was alive and well. Foolish tears welled
in her eyes.

"I will admit that I was tested to my limits by Aunt
Farrah's caution. The forbidden is seductive and soon
becomes an obsession. But I began to see that you are
smart, funny, loyal, honest, straightforward. Your
choice of studies proves your worthiness as a mother
and my partner in business. Your passionate response
to my touch, my kisses leaves no doubt in my mind
that your wifely skills will be exceptional."

Was he talking about sex? He knew all of that because of her shameless, reckless abandon when he'd
kissed her? The memories made her shiver, but she
had to concentrate. His offer would give her everything she'd always wanted. But he'd left out one very
important thing.

"Do you love me?"

He frowned into his empty champagne glass.
"What does love have to do with it? Why complicate
the perfect relationship? We will be very good together. You must marry me."

"Just what I wanted to hear." So, he didn't now,
nor could he ever love her. She met his gaze even as
she felt her eyes well with tears.

The lines of his face hardened as he pointed at her.
"I order you not to cry."

"You think you can get everything you want by
issuing an order or throwing money around?" She
stood and realized she was only wearing one shoe—
unbalanced literally and emotionally.

The moisture she'd been trying to blink away
spilled over her lower lids and trickled down her
cheeks. After brushing it away, she held out her hands
and let the light catch the shine of wetness on her

fingertips. "See? Even you can't issue an executive order and get everything you want. You're just like the rest of us mortals who put their pants on one leg at a time. You can't buy love. It must be genuine and freely given. Let me make myself perfectly clear, Your Highness. I would rather eat glass than be your wife."

There was an exit line if she'd ever heard one. But she couldn't resist just one more thing. "But what I regret the most is that now I may never open a pre-school in my mother's memory."

She walked to the foyer with all the dignity she could muster and out the door into the hall. Then she kicked off her other shoe, bent to pick it up and ran as fast as she could. Half of her hoped he would follow and try to stop her, but he didn't. Maybe it was just as well since she preferred complete privacy when she cried her eyes out.

"What did you do to Penny?"

The morning after his disastrous evening with his assistant—correction—former assistant, Rafiq stood aside as his aunt swept into his suite. As always she was impeccably groomed, her dark hair neat around her subtly made-up face. Her designer suit was stylish with its black skirt and fitted jacket composed of jewel colors—ruby, emerald and sapphire.

"I do not understand. Why would you think I have done anything to her?"

He'd spent a sleepless night trying to comprehend what had gone wrong. The incident and Penny's last words had produced a profound aching emptiness in-side him that he'd never experienced before and deeply detested now. And for God's sake, why had she asked if he loved her?

"Of course you've done something," his aunt said.

"If anyone has been wronged, it's me," he answered, tapping his chest.

"Pray tell how have you been compromised?" she asked, a skeptical tone to her voice.

That, and the accompanying look angered him. Penny's cutting words would be branded into his brain forever. "She refused to marry me."

"Why—that's wonderful." His aunt's stern expression softened, giving way to a smile of genuine pleasure.

He shook his head as if that would clear it. "I do not understand. She insulted me and you call that wonderful?"

Farrah tilted her head slightly as she studied him. "Did it ever occur to you that you've put off taking a wife because secretly you've been waiting to fall in love?"

"No." Until he'd met Penny Doyle his life had been perfectly serene, if a bit empty. But wild Arabian stallions would not pull that admission from him.

"Let me tell you what I see. You are someone who must be in the spotlight. Even as a child, you demanded your fair share and refused to be pushed aside by your brothers. In addition, you need to be in control and you think you're always right."

"I am."

Ignoring him, she continued. "Every woman who attracted your attention was like that, too. In such an infertile environment, love cannot grow. Your relationships were doomed to failure. It's why I finally had to step in."

"I don't understand."

"I knew Penny would be perfect for you."

"What are you talking about?"

"When I met her in New York the employment position for which she was applying had been filled." His aunt walked into the living room and sat on the edge of the sofa, tucking one foot behind the other ankle.

"I know all this," he said, following. He folded his arms over his chest as he looked down at her. On the coffee table between them rested Penny's satin pump. The sight of it sent a sharp pain through his chest, as if the high, sharp heel had pierced his heart.

"You also know I find her to be a breath of fresh air. When I met her, the more I talked with her the more I knew she would be just the one for you. Someone to soften your sharp edges, yet strong enough that you couldn't walk all over her."

He was beginning to see a conspiracy. "Does my father know anything about this?"

"My brother and I are in complete harmony."

"So when he appropriated my assistant, it was to make a place for Penny?"

"Yes. A brilliant strategy if I do say so myself."

"I was under the impression arranged marriages for the royal family are a thing of the past. Am I mistaken? They are alive and well and flourishing in El Zafir?"

One of her delicately shaped eyebrows rose imperiously. "If my brother's sons weren't so stubborn and obtuse, no interference would be necessary."

"So Fariq and Kamal can expect—"

"Some gentle assistance," she finished for him. "I think the situation with your brother Fariq and the nanny is progressing nicely. And if you so much as breathe a word of this to him, you will regret it."

He didn't quite know how she could make that happen, but his aunt did not issue idle threats. "I will say nothing."

"Good. Now I just have to persuade the American nurse—Ali Matlock—to accept the hospital position that Kamal offered her."

"All well and good, Aunt. But I honored Penny with a proposal of marriage. I do not see that I am deserving of blame."

"The dear child just left me. She was barely able to hold back her tears."

His insides twisted with anger. "Did someone hurt her? Tell me who, and I will make the jackal pay."

"I believe it was you. And judging by the way you look, the price is high. You really must get some sleep, Rafiq. And your appearance—" She shook her head and tsked. "What did you say to her?"

"I told her she is sensible, smart, funny, loyal, honest and capable of being trained. She would make an exceptional wife and mother."

"What about love?"

"Why are you women obsessed with such a nebulous emotion?" Annoyance shot through him. "I don't see what that has to do with it."

His aunt heaved a sigh. "No wonder she begged me to rip up her employment contract so that she could return to the United States."

The empty feeling inside him grew wider and the pain of it nearly doubled him over. "She is leaving?"

"So she says."

He rubbed a hand across his neck and turned away. "Nephew? Are you ill?"

He shook his head, then turned back to meet her gaze. "No."

She stood and went to him, putting her hand on his arm. "What is it?"

"I don't know. There is a pain. I have never felt it before. It's as if a great blackness opened up inside me. I feel as if it will swallow me, shutting out the light. What is this—thing?"

"You are the prince of toads." Aunt Farrah gave him a pitying look.

Rafiq ran his fingers through his hair and tried to curb his frustration. "I do not believe insults, no matter how clever, are especially helpful."

"I apologize—though it was irresistible. What is it I can do for you?"

"Explain to me what this awful feeling is."

"Why—it is love."

He was stunned. "I do not believe you."

"I was afraid of this." She sighed and returned to the sofa. "I know you have always believed that one woman is like the rest. But that isn't true. Love is finding the one for you, the one who is so different you cannot forget her. For some time now I've worried you would be alone."

"And you stepped in?" By bringing him Penny. Just the thought of her leaving made his stomach clench and settled a heaviness on his chest.

"Just so."

"Explain to me then why you informed her that you'd forbidden me to touch her."

"She asked."

"Which she wouldn't have if you hadn't said as much in front of her."

She shrugged. "I had to move things along. You were getting nowhere."

"Apparently, I'm doomed to be nowhere forever,"

he said, resting his hands on his hips. He would do his best to never admit it, but his aunt could be right. Loving Penny was the only explanation for his profound pain. But what could he do about it? "She asked if I loved her."

"And what did you say?"

It was his turn to sigh. "I told her love would only complicate our perfect relationship. I said we would be good together, and then I ordered her to marry me."

"Oh, dear. What did she say?"

"That she would rather eat glass than be my wife."

Aunt Farrah flinched, then shook her head in sympathy. "Poor Rafiq."

"I do not need your pity, Aunt. I need your help. You started this, as they say. What should I do?" Anger raged through him as he recalled Penny's words. "She accused me of being worse than the man who took her money."

"Oh, dear. Your crime was not recognizing love. And our Penny knew the sweetness of a mother's affection but it was taken from her far too soon. She recognizes love, but is fearful of accepting it, because the pain of losing it is too profound." She shook her head. "You are quite a pair."

"That isn't especially helpful, Aunt Farrah."

"You must go to her and stop her from leaving."

"How?"

"Tell her what's really and truly in your heart. You are the only one who knows what you feel." She stood and walked over to him. Cupping his face between her hands, she pulled him down for a kiss on the cheek. "Good luck, Nephew."

When she was gone, Rafiq continued to stare at

Penny's shoe. Quite a pair, his aunt had said. He needed his assistant. She was food for his soul and as necessary as the air he breathed. He picked up the pump.

"You and I both have a problem," he said, tracing the smooth satin with one finger. "We are useless without the perfect mate."

Chapter Twelve

Penny removed her glasses and tried to rub the grit from her eyes. Not sleeping all night did that to a girl. How fitting that she was leaving El Zafir in just about the same condition as she'd arrived. There should have been something satisfying about coming full circle. Well, not quite full.

She'd fallen asleep in the office. Rafiq had offered marriage without emotional commitment. There was something not quite equal in the two humiliations. The first had upset her dignity, the second had broken her heart.

Her first day had been filled with the exhilaration of fulfilling her dream to start a preschool in her mother's name. The following days she'd begun to hope for her own fairy tale. Both fantasies had disappeared at the stroke of midnight—or more to the point had been ripped apart when she realized Rafiq didn't love her and never could.

She stood at the French door, looking into the gar-

den below her balcony. She'd grown to love El Zafir—
the country, the people, the members of the royal family. Saying goodbye to Princess Farrah had been more
difficult than she'd anticipated.

And then there was Rafiq.

It would tear her apart to leave. But she couldn't
stay. Sighing, she remembered her words to him last
night—that she might never achieve her dream. She
wouldn't let a personal misstep keep her from a goal
she'd cherished for as long as she could remember. It
would just require more sacrifice, dedication and in-
genuity. Earning the start-up capital would take so
much longer without the employment incentives offered by El Zafir. But Penny was sure her mother
would understand that staying, seeing Rafiq and knowing he could never return her feelings, was more than
she could bear.

A knock sounded on her door. She'd called for
someone to take her bags to the car. That was probably
an attendant. On her way through the living room, she
noticed the black lace dress she hadn't persuaded herself to wear the previous night carelessly tossed over
a chair. She gazed at it and instantly tears burned at
the backs of her eyes. She'd felt beautiful in that dress.
Or maybe it was the expression in Rafiq's eyes when
he'd looked at her.

She blinked furiously but the moisture still blurred
her vision. But she was leaving. Why should she care
if she was a blubbering mess when she answered the
door? She opened it, shocked to see Rafiq standing
there.

"Penny," he said.

He looked terrible. He looked like she felt, as if he
hadn't slept in days. His slacks were wrinkled. So was

the white shirt with the sleeves rolled to just below his elbows. Stubble darkened his cheeks and jaw. She'd never seen him anything less than impeccably groomed—hardly even a hint of a crease in his slacks, let alone not cleanly shaven. Was it what she'd said last night? Pity started to creep in. It took every ounce of her strength, but she managed to bite back words of apology.

"Your Highness."

"Since when do you address me in such a formal manner?" he asked, moving into the entryway.

"It's better than 'Your Worship.'" She was being a smart aleck. It was her last means of defense.

"Indeed it is." He stood with his hands behind his back and glanced down at her suitcases. "Please close the door."

"Is that an order?"

"It is if that's the only way I can compel you to obey."

She closed the door. "What is it you want? I didn't think we had more to say."

He pulled her satin pump from behind his back. "You left this."

"Thank you," she said. "Although it wasn't necessary to return it. I left the other one in the bedroom."

He set it on a table beside the door. "Its mate?"

"Yes," she said. "Along with the rest of the clothes that are part of the job. I'd love to stick around and see your assistant in some of those numbers. He's probably—"

"Not your size," he interrupted. "You were going to leave without saying goodbye." Anger laced his words.

"We said everything there was to say last night."

He shook his head. "Hardly."

"What else is there?"

"I have secured in your name the land you wanted for the preschool."

"Why should I believe you?"

He pulled an envelope from his coat pocket and held it out. "The papers are in here, including names and phone numbers of the agent who negotiated the transaction and the bank representative who is handling the account for construction, start-up and operation."

With shaking fingers, she took it and glanced through the paperwork. It was all there. "You're giving me my preschool?"

He shrugged. "It is important to you."

"But why? After what I said—"

"My aunt has grown fond of you. She blames me for your hasty departure. And the fact that I've deprived her of an able and amusing assistant."

Penny turned away, hiding the tears that sprang to her eyes again. "I will miss Princess Farrah very much."

"Is there anyone else you will miss?"

You, she wanted to say. But she couldn't and still maintain her dignity. "I regret that I must leave before my contract is fulfilled. But the princess understood and said she wouldn't force me to stay if I was unhappy."

"Are you?" When she didn't comment he said, "I wish to see your face, your eyes. Turn around. Look at me, Penny."

She shook her head. "I need to go home."

"This is your home."

"No."

He moved behind her, barely touching. Every nerve ending in her body hummed with anticipation. She could feel the heat of his body, his warm breath stirring her hair. His strong hands curved around her upper arms and she wanted to lean into his strength. Instead, she let him turn her to face him.

"They say home is where the heart is. I want to hear from your own lips that it is not here." His dark eyes burned into hers. "You will not lie. I know you too well. Tell me you would not leave your heart behind—with me—when you return to the United States."

Again she blinked, trying to dispel the moisture she didn't want him to see. "I have fond memories of my time in El Zafir."

"I do not wish you to leave." There was a note of desperation in his voice.

"Staying is out of the question."

"That is absurd. Of course you can stay. I have asked you to be my wife."

"I can't. I never thought I could have the fairy tale. Now I know settling for anything less would be a mistake."

"You cannot go," he said again. "If you do I will be Penny-less."

"That's ridiculous. You've got everything money can buy. And enough money to buy whatever you want that you don't have."

"All I have is a terrible pain here," he said, putting a fist over his chest. "It is where my heart used to be."

"Used to be?" she asked.

He nodded. "It has been stolen."

All her senses went on alert. It was stupid, but her hope quotient shot up.

"By who? Or is it whom?"

"You." He took her in his arms. "The only time I am whole is when I hold you."

She was awfully glad he was holding her, because her head was spinning. But her heart… Hope, desire, expectation longing, all of that was growing in her despite her warnings. "Please don't toy with me."

"Never. You are correct. I have money to purchase anything I desire. But there is something you must understand. I desire you. But there is only one Penny Doyle and that makes you priceless. My desert jewel."

"I don't know what to say—"

"It's simple. Tell me you will stay and take away this terrible pain."

He still hadn't said what she wanted—no, needed—to hear. If she gave in without it, she sensed their relationship would never be on a level playing field. He was right. Material belongings meant very little, but emotional commitment was irreplaceable. She refused to be satisfied with anything less than hearing him say the words.

"I'm sorry to cause you any discomfort," she said. "But I have heard nothing that compels me to stay. Under the circumstances, to do so would maximize my own distress."

"Ah," he said. There was humor and male satisfaction in that single, small syllable. It was the sound of a man who knew what he had to do to get what he wanted.

But Penny had grown to know this man well. He would say nothing if it wasn't the truth. Her future happiness hung in the balance and she held her breath.

"You want tender words." He looked into her eyes. "Do you remember when you asked me if there was anything I wasn't good at?"

"Yes," she said.

"I have discovered I am not good at love."

"Do tell." She couldn't help smiling. The words were chocolate to a sweets-deprived soul. "So are you ready yet to admit that love is important? Not just a complication made up by women to vex men?"

He smiled. "It was too much to hope you had forgotten my careless words." Then he grew serious. "I will admit only that I love you."

"Oh, Rafiq—" She tried to step back, to better see his expression.

His grip tightened as his eyes smoldered. "You have not yet said how you feel about me."

"Yes—surely I did. You must know."

"No. You have only said you would rather eat glass than be my wife. I am new at this love business. I find it would be most beneficial to hear the words." He cupped her cheek in the warm palm of his hand. "Tell me you love me, Penny. I think I see it in your eyes. Tell me I'm right. I must hear *you* say it."

"I love you, Rafiq. I think I loved you from the first moment I saw you, before I knew you were a prince."

He closed his eyes for a moment and pulled her to him in a relentlessly fierce embrace. "I am glad. So you will stay?"

"As your assistant?"

Laughter rumbled in his chest. "I think we have done this before. I did not like your answer."

"Try me again. I think there's magic in the air tonight."

He set her away from him then took her hand and

grabbed her high-heeled shoe from the table beside them. "Come with me."

Anywhere, she wanted to say.

He led her into the living room and gently urged her onto the couch. Then he went down on one knee and cupped her ankle in his hand. Slipping off her sensible brown shoe, he said, "Penny Doyle, will you marry me?"

She looked at him. "I'm new at this, too, but in books and movies when someone proposes, he slips something on. Usually a ring."

"In the fairy tale, the maiden whose foot fits the glass slipper must marry the prince," he said, easily sliding the black satin pump on her foot. "It looks like a perfect fit to me."

"It's my shoe. Of course it fits."

"I do not wish to take a chance. The outcome is far too important to me. Do not keep me in suspense. I love you. Will you do me the honor of being my wife?"

Penny slid off the sofa and knelt in front of him. "I would be honored to be your wife. But I have one request."

"I understand that you want to oversee starting the preschool. If you'd like we can honeymoon in the States and I will help you. And when we return to El Zafir, I would insist the king make you minister of early childhood education and preschool development in this country. Women work here, too, and need to care for their children."

Her heart was so full of love for this man she thought she would burst with happiness. This was more than she'd ever dared to dream. "I accept. But that isn't what I was going to ask."

"What is it you require?"

"I require you to kiss me at least once a day the way you did in the garden the night of the charity ball. You made me believe in fairy tales. I want to live it for the rest of our lives."

"How very fortunate for me that I can deny you nothing." He smiled, a smile filled with tenderness and love. "It will be my pleasure to make all your dreams come true for eternity."

Then Rafiq Hassan, Prince of El Zafir, Minister of Domestic and Foreign Affairs took Penny Doyle, soon to be his desert bride into his arms and kissed her, sealing his promise of happily ever after.

*   *   *   *   *

*Look for the story of
nanny Crystal Rawlins
and single father Fariq Hassan in
TO KISS A SHEIK (SR1686),
the second book in Teresa Southwick's
exciting new miniseries,
DESERT BRIDES.
On sale September 2003.*

eHARLEQUIN.com

Looking for today's most popular
books at great prices?
At www.eHarlequin.com, we offer:

- An **extensive selection** of romance
  books by top authors!

- **New** releases, Themed Collections
  and hard-to-find **backlist.**

- A sneak peek at Upcoming books.

- Enticing book **excerpts** and **back
  cover copy!**

- Read recommendations from other
  readers (and post your own)!

- Find out what everybody's reading
  in **Bestsellers.**

- **Save BIG** with everyday discounts
  and exclusive online offers!

- Easy, convenient **24-hour shopping.**

- Our **Romance Legend** will help select
  reading that's *exactly* right for you!

**Your purchases are 100%
guaranteed—so shop online
at www.eHarlequin.com today!**

If you enjoyed what you just read,
then we've got an offer you can't resist!

Take 2 bestselling love stories FREE!

Plus get a FREE surprise gift!

Clip this page and mail it to Silhouette Reader Service™

IN U.S.A.	IN CANADA
3010 Walden Ave.	P.O. Box 609
P.O. Box 1867	Fort Erie, Ontario
Buffalo, N.Y. 14240-1867	L2A 5X3

YES! Please send me 2 free Silhouette Romance® novels and my free surprise gift. After receiving them, if I don't wish to receive anymore, I can return the shipping statement marked cancel. If I don't cancel, I will receive 6 brand-new novels every month, before they're available in stores! In the U.S.A., bill me at the bargain price of $3.34 plus 25¢ shipping and handling per book and applicable sales tax, if any*. In Canada, bill me at the bargain price of $3.80 plus 25¢ shipping and handling per book and applicable taxes**. That's the complete price and a savings of at least 10% off the cover prices—what a great deal! I understand that accepting the 2 free books and gift places me under no obligation ever to buy any books. I can always return a shipment and cancel at any time. Even if I never buy another book from Silhouette, the 2 free books and gift are mine to keep forever.

215 SDN DNUM
315 SDN DNUN

Name	(PLEASE PRINT)	
Address	Apt.#	
City	State/Prov.	Zip/Postal Code

* Terms and prices subject to change without notice. Sales tax applicable in N.Y.
** Canadian residents will be charged applicable provincial taxes and GST.
   All orders subject to approval. Offer limited to one per household and not valid to
   current Silhouette Romance® subscribers.
   ® are registered trademarks of Harlequin Books S.A., used under license.

SROM02   ©1998 Harlequin Enterprises Limited

SILHOUETTE *Romance*®

COMING NEXT MONTH

#1678 BEAUTY & THE BEASTLY RANCHER—
Judy Christenberry
From the Circle K

Anna Pointer agreed to a marriage of convenience for the sake of her kids. After all, Joe Crawford was kind, generous—her children loved him—and he was handsome, too! But Joe thought he could only offer his money and his name. Could Anna convince her husband that he was her Prince Charming?

#1679 DISTRACTING DAD—Terry Essig

Nothing encourages romance like…*a flood?* When Nate Parker's dad accidentally flooded Allie MacLord's apartment, Nate let his beautiful neighbor bunk with him—but he had no intention of falling in love. But then neighborly affection included Allie's sweet kisses….

#1680 JARED'S TEXAS HOMECOMING—
Patricia Thayer
The Texas Brotherhood

Jared Trager went to Texas to find his deceased brother's son—and became a stepfather to the boy! Dana Shayne thought Jared was a guardian angel sent to save her farm and her heart. But could she forgive his deceit when she learned his true intentions?

#1681 DID YOU SAY…*WIFE?*—Judith McWilliams

Secretary Joselyn Stemic was secretly in love with Lucas Tarrington—her sexy boss! So when an accident left Lucas with amnesia, she pretended to be his wife. At first it was just so the hospital would let her care for him—but what would happen when she took her "husband" home?

#1682 MARRIED IN A MONTH—Linda Goodnight

Love-shy rancher Colt Garret didn't know a thing about babies and never wanted a wife. Then he received custody of a two-month-old and desperately turned to Kati Winslow for help. Kati agreed to be the nanny for baby Evan…if Colt agreed to marry her in a month!

#1683 DAD TODAY, GROOM TOMORROW—Holly Jacobs
Perry Square

Louisa Clancy had left home eight years ago with a big check and an even bigger secret. She'd thought she put the past behind her—then Joe Delacamp came into her store and spotted *their* son. Was this long-lost love about to threaten all Louisa's dreams? Or would it fulfill her deepest longings…?

SRCNM0703